LOVE ON TRACK

Flora Petersen surprises family and friends when she successfully applies for a job as a train manager. Though nervous to begin with, she soon finds herself enjoying the daily routine of assisting passengers — including one she privately nicknames 'Mr Gorgeous'. Jack, father of a small daughter, commutes to his job via train. Since his wife died, he's had no time for romance. Until one day he notices the lovely woman who sells him a ticket, and realises he's seen her somewhere before . . .

Books by *Jill Barry*
in the *Linford Romance Library:*

JILL BARRY

◆

LOVE ON
TRACK

Complete and Unabridged

LINFORD
Leicester

First published in Great Britain in 2017

First Linford Edition
published 2018

A catalogue record for this book is available
from the British Library.

ISBN 978–1–4448–3714–8

Published by
F. A. Thorpe (Publishing)
Anstey, Leicestershire

Set by Words & Graphics Ltd.
Anstey, Leicestershire
Printed and bound in Great Britain by
T. J. International Ltd., Padstow, Cornwall

This book is printed on acid-free paper

1

'Daddy, Daddy! I've lost Freddie. Where is he? I need him!'

Flora Petersen stopped gazing through the train carriage window. Two rows in front, a fair-haired man was on his feet, a puzzled expression on his face. It was, Flora decided, a rather attractive face.

'He must be here somewhere, Ellie. Teddy bears don't go walkabout. Let's look on the floor.' The child's father disappeared from view while the train slowed down, ready to stop at the next station.

Flora held her breath. The little girl began twisting one of her blonde corkscrew curls, but Freddie appeared to be playing hard to get.

'Sweetheart, we have to get off here.' Mr Gorgeous — as Flora couldn't resist nicknaming him — uncurled himself.

'We can't delay the train. Maybe you left Freddie in the toilet? I'll speak to the guard and leave my phone number.'

'Nooo!' The child sounded heartbroken. 'We can't go without Freddie. He'll be lonely without me.'

Flora, still recalling the anguish of losing a treasured cuddly bunny toy, couldn't ignore this crisis. She bent over, wondering whether Freddie was lurking beneath her seat. At first, she saw nothing but a discarded crisp packet; then, as the train lurched, a smiling brown bear slid into view. Flora reached out and grabbed Freddie just as the train rocked, tipping her sideways so she landed on her knees in the aisle. Thank goodness she was wearing trousers.

'Are you alright?' Mr Gorgeous moved closer, looking at her, his expression concerned.

Flora held the little bear aloft. 'I'm fine, thank you. Is this what you're looking for?'

The little girl gave a delighted yell

and her father held out his hand, either to take the bear or to help Flora to her feet. Aware of her crimson cheeks, she scrambled up, handing Freddie over with as much dignity as possible.

'I suppose my daughter must have dropped him and the train's motion sent him your way. You've definitely saved the day! Thank you.'

His smile lit up his face. His eyes were the bluest blue. Why, oh why, were the nicest men always spoken for?

* * *

Auntie Marion, looking casual in a rainbow-striped woollen jumper over black jeans, was waiting when Flora hauled her wheelie case onto the platform at Bell's Hill.

Her aunt hurried towards her. 'Here you are!' She flung her arms around Flora.

'You're looking good, Auntie.' Flora breathed in the scent of sandalwood soap, a perfume she always associated with her mum's sister.

'And you, my dear, look a million dollars, as they say! How long is it since I saw you last? And did you buy that beautiful leather jacket at a discount? That sea-green really brings out the colour of your eyes.'

Flora, released from her aunt's embrace, began pushing her case towards the exit. 'Thank you. It must be a year or so since we last got together. And yes, I did buy my jacket at a special price. I'm sorry not to have visited before, but you know how it is.'

'There's no need to apologise. Your job has kept you busy, and I've done a bit of travelling over the last months. But I was sad to hear about the shop closure. Your mum said you were pretty cut up over it.'

'Yes, I was. But as soon as my boss decided to close the menswear department, I knew our days were numbered. In the end, there was only myself left for me to manage!'

Marion pointed to a small red car.

'That's Cherry. She's new since I last came to see you. Let's get going, and you can tell me more while we drive home.'

Flora lifted her luggage into the boot. 'It's so kind of you to invite me to stay. Mum's probably fed up of me hanging round the place, trying to decide what kind of job I want.'

'Knowing your mother, I doubt that! But I do know she hopes you won't decide to follow your elder brother to Canada.'

Flora laughed as she settled into the passenger seat. 'No chance. I'd love to visit him one day, but Grant's always been more adventurous than me.'

'I don't suppose there's any chance the people who bought the business would keep you on, if only while they settle in?'

'None at all. The new owners have applied for change of use so they can start up a health store.'

'They must reckon that's more profitable than running a small town draper's?'

Flora smiled at her aunt's use of the old-fashioned word. 'So many people shop online these days, or travel to Ashfield. They've got a great shopping precinct now, with all the high-street chain stores you'd expect.'

'And I suppose people are more inclined to take their health seriously in this enlightened age of ours! Couldn't you do some kind of course and work for the new people?'

'The buyers are a married couple who plan to run the place together with part-time help later on. I need to find a full-time job.'

'If I can be of help, just say the word,' Marion said. 'Don't forget, I used to be a personnel manager back in the day.'

'What we call Human Resources now?'

'Humph! Why does everything have to be given a new title nowadays?' Marion indicated to overtake a tractor chugging along in front while Flora thought back to when her aunt had worked for a big department store chain in its London offices. She'd never married, and on retirement had returned to West Wales to care for her mum, Flora's grandmother.

'You must have dealt with an unbelievable number of people over the years,' Flora said.

'But I loved my job — I enjoyed slotting people into the right places.' Marion glanced swiftly at her niece. 'I'm not sure I'd have put you in the fashion department, though.'

'Thanks a bundle, Auntie! It's a good job I'm fond of you.'

'Me and my big mouth! You must have been good at your job for them to make you their manager. No, what I had in mind was something where your skills of tact and diplomacy would be important, not to mention your voice.'

'Sorry?' Flora felt puzzled.

'Customer Services would be an excellent place for you. I always remember how good you were at sorting out family arguments.'

Flora chuckled. 'Grant and Dad were

a real pain sometimes when they used to fight over who should take charge of the remote control. I was only trying to keep the peace.'

'Precisely. I also recall your mum saying you were always a tactful child. It's a good skill to have, Flora, so why don't you play to your strengths? Didn't you walk into that dress shop job by chance?'

'I was sixteen, and dithering over going to sixth-form college; but when I saw the job vacancy advertised, I decided to apply. When they offered me the job, I took it, thinking that if I wanted to study for A-levels, I could always resign at the end of that summer. Somehow, college flew through the window, and my boss must've thought I had something about me because I ended up working for her for the next seven years.'

Aunt Marion navigated the round-about at the end of the dual carriageway and turned down the side road leading to her house. 'Well, maybe losing your job at this stage of your life could turn out to be a blessing in disguise!'

'Do you mean there's more chance of picking up a seasonal job in the spring? There aren't too many of those down our way.'

Her chauffeur turned into her driveway and brought the car to a smooth halt. She turned to Flora. 'I really meant, this is a time to explore your options and decide what you really want to do. The teenage Flora was a very different person from the young woman she is today. And, whatever your mother might say, this could be your chance to reinvent yourself.'

Flora frowned. 'Reinvent myself? Am I that boring?'

'Of course not, but at your age, you should be seeking new horizons. And from what I recall, your GCSE grades were pretty darned good.'

'But I like the little world I'm part of,' Flora said. 'I have a lovely home, some nice friends, and then there's — well, there's Tom.'

'That young farmer? He's still around, then?' Marion sounded disapproving.

'Yes, but Tom's not such a young farmer nowadays! We still have a sort of understanding, though.'

Her aunt shot her a very strange look. 'Let's go and put the kettle on. I even made a cake in your honour.'

'I'm impressed.' Flora's aunt wasn't known for her baking skills.

'You can be my guinea-pig.' Marion opened her door.

Flora followed suit. 'Why, are you entering a cake in the village fete or something?'

'No way.' Suddenly Flora's aunt seemed lost for words. 'I've, um . . . well, I seem to have acquired a gentleman friend.'

Flora laughed out loud. 'Goodness me, talk about a dark horse, Auntie. I thought your opinion of men was zero.'

'Only in some cases, my dear. This one's our new vicar, who happens to be a widower. We get on very well, but he's partial to a bit of homemade cake.'

Flora rolled her eyes. 'Don't tell me you have rivals for his affections — widows plying him with lemon drizzles and Swiss rolls!'

'I don't think so. But I noticed his face fall when I unwrapped a carrot cake from a certain well-known super-market — and, for the first time in years, I found myself determined to impress him next time he called. I must be going soft in my old age!'

* * *

That evening, after Flora insisted on washing up, she joined her aunt in the small conservatory Marion had added to the house. There was still some sunshine, and as Flora sank down on the window-seat, she admired a lilac tree dripping with blossoms. Nearby, swathes of purple and white tulips covered the grassy bank.

'Your garden shows how much you love it,' she said, accepting a glass of homemade rhubarb wine.

'It probably proves that your mother got the baking gene while I inherited the green fingers.'

'From Gran, you mean?'

'Your maternal grandmother, yes.'

'So what do you think I inherited?'

'Those beautiful green eyes and slender figure.'

'Well, thank you . . . but I really meant talent or personality.'

'Your gran was what we'd call a people person, nowadays. You're much better at talking to strangers than your mum is.'

'But you must follow Gran, considering you worked most of your life in Human Resources?'

Aunt Marion sniffed. 'Still can't get used to the term but, yes, I suppose you're right.'

'To be honest, I don't think I want to go back to studying. Not even to get a qualification like yours.'

'You could handle a training course, though?'

'Of course, provided it would lead to something I really wanted to do. Dad says I'm being fussy but now the shop's gone, I feel as if I should look for something a bit more demanding.'

Marion sipped her wine. 'Exactly my thoughts. You know I travel by train sometimes?'

'Yes, I do.'

'Well, last time I used the local line, I got chatting to the train manager.'

'You always did enjoy talking to strangers.'

'Ha! Well, this one happened to be a very pleasant young woman.'

'Really? We don't see too many female conductors, do we?'

'Which is why I'm raising the subject. It didn't occur to me at the time, because you were still working at the dress shop, but I think I might have happened upon the perfect career choice for you!'

2

Flora sat back in her seat and gazed out at the changing landscape. Last time she'd travelled this route, she'd been off to visit her aunt. On returning, she'd done some research, and — not without a little apprehension — filled in her online application for the position of train conductor. The resulting telephone interview must have gone well, because now she was off to meet her fate! If she passed this test, she would be starting her training.

Her father was amused by her decision. 'Swipe me!' he'd said, when she'd told her parents.

Her mum's face had been a picture! 'It sounds a weird sort of life to me,' she told Flora. 'Hours spent on a train, issuing tickets, checking them, rattling along for miles! Are you sure about this, love? You get some funny people about these days. What does Tom think?'

Flora smiled to herself. She hadn't told her mother that if she got this job, she'd have the perfect excuse not to spend what she considered duty dates with farmer Tom. It was high time he stopped taking her for granted, and found some other girl to settle down with. She'd also reassured her mother that the railway company looked after its employees, training them to cope with difficult situations, and ensuring proper breaks and accommodation were supplied should it ever be necessary to stop overnight.

Flora intended to take note of the female train conductor's movements on this journey. After all, she was travelling all the way to Parkswell for her interview, so it was a good chance to observe.

When the young woman arrived to check her ticket, Flora looked at her name badge and produced her special travel warrant, receiving a big smile in return.

'Good morning,' Trudy said. 'I haven't noticed you on this route before. Are you having a day out in Parkswell?'

Flora lowered her voice. 'I'm going for an interview at the railway offices. I'm to see someone called Sam Jones.'

Trudy nodded. 'I know Sam. What position have you applied for?'

'The same job you're doing!'

'Oh, wow, good for you,' Trudy said. 'I wondered if you were looking to work at Head Office.'

'I'm not sure I could settle into an office routine. I used to manage a dress shop, and liked having all the different customers coming in, especially when they were looking for clothes for weddings and holidays.'

'So why did you leave?'

'The shop ceased trading.'

'Aw, I'm sorry. What made you apply for this job?'

'The thought of working on a train hadn't even occurred to me until my aunt came up with it.'

'Good for her. I used to work as

16

cabin crew, flying out of Cardiff; but after ten years doing that, my partner and I decided to move back to West Wales, and hopefully start a family.' Trudy glanced behind her. 'Whoops! Must get on, or we'll reach the next stop before I can finish checking tickets. See you later.'

Flora wanted to ask questions, but knew she must wait. As soon as the trolley operator reached her, she asked for a coffee and flapjack biscuit. Her appointment was for one o'clock and, having not eaten much breakfast, she didn't want her rumbling tummy to deafen her interviewer.

When she left the train at Parkswell, with plenty of time left before her appointment, she lingered on the platform, watching people disembarking, talking on their phones, or checking the destination boards. She turned in surprise as someone appeared at her side.

'Hi! Sorry we didn't get a chance to chat again, but I just wanted to wish you luck. Can you find the way all right?' Trudy asked. 'I'm sorry, I should ask you what your name is.'

'It's Flora, and I think I need to go out the main entrance, turn left, and go through the big doors of the next building along.'

'Perfect. I'm off back down the route after my break, so I'll probably not see you later, but I hope our paths will cross in the future.'

'Me too. Thanks, Trudy.'

Flora watched her new acquaintance pull out a small notepad and pen from her jacket pocket.

'I've just had a thought,' Trudy said. 'If I scribble my email address down, you can contact me if you have any questions — or, hopefully, to tell me you've been accepted for training.'

'That's brilliant.' Flora waited until the other girl handed over her contact details. 'I promise to let you know one way or the other.'

*　*　*

Passengers stood around, sitting on benches, pushing their luggage, heading for the shop — generally behaving, Flora thought, as if there was nothing momentous about this particular day. Little did they know this fledgling railway employee was facing her first appearance before the travelling public, making today a very special one for her.

'I can't help feeling nervous,' Flora said as she walked with Trudy towards the train's rear. She'd enjoyed her training course, but now the stabilisers were well and truly off.

'That's understandable,' Trudy said. 'I'm glad we kept in touch, and now we'll be working the same routes for a while, even if we only have time for a quick catch-up before trundling off again.'

'If I ever have the courage to make it solo,' Flora said gloomily.

'Of course you will, silly.' Trudy pushed down the door handle. 'Here we go. I'll show you where to stow your bag, and we'll take it from there.'

Flora took a deep breath. 'Do you remember your first day on the schedule?'

'Will I ever forget it!'

'I bet you had no trouble at all — after those years working for an airline.'

'Actually, I was really slow at ticketing. I nearly handed in my notice at one point, even though I loved the rest of the job. Luckily, I got the hang of things, and here I am.'

'I can't imagine you being anything but efficient.' Flora followed Trudy into the conductor's office and looked round. 'Maybe I could hide in here if I do something stupid.'

'The best way is to get out there and go for it. I'll be with you all the time, and you're going to meet some lovely people. We have lots of regular passengers on this route, believe me.'

For one brief moment, Flora remembered the lost teddy bear incident and pictured the harassed dad and his little girl. Was Mr Gorgeous one of those regular passengers? She'd pictured his curly fair hair and blue eyes far too often! Now she pushed the thought away. Even if he travelled every day, he was quite obviously a family man.

'Right,' said Trudy. 'I'm going to ask you to walk the length of the train — only three carriages, so don't look so worried! We need to check everywhere is clean and tidy, so don't forget the loos. Our cleaners are very good, but we're all human. Oh, and take some spare safety leaflets in case you find a seat which hasn't got one. I'll follow you and put tags on the reserved seats, though there aren't many of them on this service.'

Time flew. The big trolley with its assortment of refreshments was trundled up the ramp and on board ready for departure. Trudy and the driver agreed they were ready for the station announcement to be made.

'With all those doors, we can't welcome everyone on board,' Trudy explained. 'But I usually hover outside on the platform while they're getting on. Like now!'

Flora hung around too, managing to murmur good-morning greetings and smile at people. Wearing her smart dark blue uniform helped her confidence, and between them, she and Trudy assisted an elderly gentleman with his suitcase and a big bag he told them contained his golf clubs.

Before long, doors were banging. People were settling into their seats and Trudy, having signalled to the train dispatcher on the platform, hopped back on board. Whistles were blown and they were off.

'You can make the first announcement,' said Trudy.

All of a sudden, something strange and wonderful happened. Flora thought back to Auntie Marion's compliment about her voice and, banishing her nerves, began looking forward to helping make the passengers' journey enjoyable.

'Good morning, my name is Flora . . . ' she began.

'Well done,' Trudy said after she finished. 'You may as well check everyone has a ticket now.' She grinned. 'Oh, I'm such a slave-driver.'

'Just don't fly out of a window,' Flora said. 'You never know when I might need you.'

★　★　★

'Well, what did you think of your first day?' Trudy asked as she and Flora trundled their wheelie cases down the platform.

'Once I stopped shaking with fright, I really enjoyed it,' Flora said.

'You were fine,' Trudy said. 'We're on the roster to work together again tomorrow. And once they let you loose on your own, you know you can always text me if something's bothering you and you don't want to talk to any of the crew.'

'That's cheered me up! I just want to do a good job and not cause any problems.'

'You seemed to be enjoying your chat with the old gentleman we helped on board this morning.'

'Oh dear, I hope I didn't spend too much time talking.'

'There are always sections where you can afford to chat with passengers, if you wish. Working on a train's very different from working as cabin crew, where you have to serve the food and drinks and sell all kinds of things.'

'At least we have no seatbelts to check, and hopefully no turbulence.'

Trudy chuckled. 'Just the constant lurching and swaying. How many bruises have you got, I wonder?'

'Tell me about it,' Flora said ruefully. 'I hope I'll get more used to dodging seats as time goes by.'

'I'm sure you will.' Trudy punched in the code and opened the door to the staff section. 'Did you drive to work today?'

'No, my dad dropped me off. I need to sort out a second-hand car. I used to walk to work at the dress shop, but our house is a bit too far from the station for that.'

'I can give you a lift back, unless your dad's already here.'

'I expect he will be, but thanks anyway.'

'Well, the offer stands for tomorrow. I pass the end of your road on the way to our house. Now, let's sign off.'

It wasn't long before the two were ready to leave.

'We're all done here, so let's call it a day,' Trudy said. 'Don't forget we're on the earlier service tomorrow morning!'

'I won't.'

'I'll introduce you to some more of my regulars.'

★   ★   ★

Jack Slater parked his car at the far end of Ashfield Station's car park and strode towards the platform entrance. He'd breathed a sigh of relief earlier when Ellie gave him a goodbye kiss and picked up her spoon again, asking her nana if they could go to the park after school. His little girl had taken a while to settle into their new surroundings, but he thanked his lucky stars that his parents had offered to give the two of them a home while he house-hunted in the area.

How long was it since he'd lost Lindy? Quickly, he counted back to the day of the car accident, calculating that it had been three years and two months now. Ellie, still toddling then, had barely any recollection of her lovely mummy; though Jack still had photographs around, hoping to keep his late wife's memory alive. Those first days had been dark ones, but his little blonde-haired daughter had kept him from going under.

On the platform, he nodded to a couple of other passengers, their faces now familiar ones. He never spoke to his fellow travellers, apart from a brief greeting; or, if the train happened to run late, to share a grumble. Today he was off to the office at Jamesbridge where he was based three days a week, working at home for the other two days.

Minutes later, the train appeared, at first a pair of headlights in the distance until it snaked towards the platform and rumbled to a halt. Jack always stood at a particular place, so he could easily access the first carriage. His work satchel slung across one shoulder, he waited patiently while a couple of people got off before jumping up the step.

Inside, he settled himself in a window seat and took out the morning paper. Jack liked a proper paper, even though his colleagues teased him about being old-fashioned. So what! He liked being old-fashioned, even though he worked in town planning as a senior consultant with all the sophisticated computer programs he needed at his fingertips.

He didn't glance up until the train conductor arrived, and he pulled out his wallet to buy a day return ticket.

'Good morning,' said the young woman.

Jack returned the greeting, but barely glanced at her as she took his cash and printed his ticket. 'Thanks for having the right money,' she said.

'Uhuh,' he said, pocketing the ticket and registering that he hadn't seen this girl on the service before, though there was often another young woman performing the same job.

He went back to his reading, but something kept niggling at his memory until he looked up again, this time paying attention to the ticket conductor's pleasing voice as she stooped beside a young woman who had a small child beside her plus a baby cuddled against her in a sling.

Where had he heard that voice before? Jack frowned and cast his mind back to the last meeting he'd attended at work, where two women had been present. No, it hadn't been then. Did she work in a shop, then? Or did she have a child at Ellie's school? Jack took his daughter to school and collected her on the days he worked at home. But, after a little more thought, he decided he hadn't found the right answer.

He turned the page of his paper. And when the conductor made her way back down the train, he looked up to find she was looking straight at him. He met her gaze and saw the same beautiful green eyes he'd noticed that day when he'd taken Ellie out, and she'd mislaid her teddy bear on the train. The attractive girl, by finding Freddie, had saved his daughter distress and her dad much hassle. This was surely the same young woman, though he hadn't connected Freddie's rescuer with the young train conductor, whose appearance in her uniform hadn't rung any bells in his brain.

He wanted to ask her if she remembered him, but told himself not to be so foolish. After all, he was only one of hundreds of passengers using that service.

3

'Flora, can you spare a moment?'

'Coming!' Flora moved swiftly down the aisle to meet Trudy at the point where the first carriage linked with the next. She'd recognised Mr Gorgeous as soon as she came face to face with him, though he obviously didn't remember her. Well, why should he? She longed to ask him how Freddie was and watch his face, but as a new girl on the service, she daren't risk a passenger judging her as being too familiar.

'I want you to meet Roman,' Trudy said. 'He's a lovely boy, and he's at Sixth Form College in Glanalan.' Trudy lowered her voice. 'He lives with his Polish grandma and English grandfather; and, amazingly for a teenager, he enjoys a chat when you get time.'

The connecting door whooshed open and a lanky boy with cropped blond hair and a big smile came through it.

'Hi again, Roman. I'd like you to meet my new colleague. Flora will probably be popping up on the morning train when I'm not.'

Roman beamed. 'Hi, Flora, it's good to meet you. I hope you enjoy working on this train.'

'I'm sure I shall,' Flora said. 'It's good to meet you too, Roman. What subjects are you studying?'

'Sciences. I hope to become a doctor one day, like my mother.'

'That's wonderful.' Flora looked up at the teenager, who towered above her. 'I hope you achieve your ambition.'

'If hard work can ensure it, I shall,' Roman said. 'But there's a long, long way to go yet.'

The train was stopping at Glanalan Station. Roman hoisted his backpack and waited for the door mechanism to allow him out.

'Goodbye, ladies,' he said, jumping on to the platform. 'Catch you later!'

'Roman's an interesting young man,'

Trudy told Flora after they'd done their bit and were pulling away again. 'He reads a lot of science fiction and comes out with some amazing stuff sometimes. It can be funny at times when we have a brief chat, then we get to his stop. The next time I see him, he continues from where we left off the time before. I really don't know how he does it.'

'It sounds perfect for someone hoping to study medicine then,' Flora said. 'He'll be able to memorise his patients' ailments, and if the computer goes down he'll just go on as usual!'

'Hmm.' Trudy didn't look convinced. 'You should run that by him and see what he says.'

Flora set off to sell tickets, and although she thought she was being slow, she didn't have any problems. She didn't notice where Mr Gorgeous left the train as Trudy insisted she got herself a coffee. The rest of the journey flew by, with passengers getting off and new ones boarding: some in work mode, others obviously off for a shopping day at Parkswell, with several making day-trips to Cardiff. On arrival at Cardiff Central Station, the two conductors left the train, looking forward to their break before setting off again later.

* * *

'There certainly isn't time to get bored doing this job,' Flora said as they sat down at a quiet table with their trays of food.

'It's the different views that I love,' Trudy said. 'Have you had a chance to notice how the landscape changes so very quickly?'

'Oh, yes.' Flora buttered a roll. 'I noticed that caravan park when I was travelling to Parkswell for my interview. There's a sloping row of ice-cream-coloured houses near the bay.'

'I know where you mean.' Trudy sipped her cup of tea. 'You can see rows of vans just along the side of the estuary. Pennock always strikes me as being a lovely place to stay.'

'You're right about the views changing,' Flora went on. 'In places, you can see industrial estates with houses in the distance; then all of a sudden we've got fields again, with cattle or sheep.'

'Don't forget the horses.'

'Ah, you mean the riding school just outside Wolf's Hill. I've noticed the sign advertising a gymkhana somewhere too.'

'Anyone would think you two had nothing to do but stare out of the window all day,' said a male voice. 'Mind if I join you?'

Flora looked up. A tall, dark-haired man, dressed in uniform, stood holding a tray while smiling down at them.

'Feel free, Gareth,' Trudy said. 'Unless you're going to be rude about us again.'

'I wouldn't dare!' Gareth's eyes twinkled as he sized up Flora. 'Sorry to interrupt your conversation, ladies, but I wanted to come and say hallo to the newbie in our midst.'

'Hello,' Flora said. 'They don't come much greener than me, but Trudy's putting up with me brilliantly.'

'Flora's hardly put a foot wrong,' Trudy said. 'Yet.'

'Give her time,' Gareth said, stirring his tea.

Flora looked from one to the other. 'Are you winding me up?'

'Definitely not! It's just that the very best of us sometimes comes up against a weird situation or makes a howler over the public address system. It's inevitable.'

'It's life,' Trudy agreed.

'So, come on,' Flora said. 'Tell me what's happened to each of you, then I shan't feel so bad when my turn comes.'

'How long have you got?' Gareth asked, checking his watch.

'Hey, you.' Trudy wrinkled her nose at him. 'Don't go putting her off. I was thrilled to bits when Flora turned up on the train one morning and told me she was going for an interview.'

'I was only teasing,' Gareth cut into a crisp rasher of bacon. 'You're very welcome, Flora. We could certainly do with a bit more glamour round here.'

'Cheek! We could also do with a few more heartthrob guards and train drivers on the route.'

'Touché! I meant, of course, present company excepted.'

'I'm still waiting for these confessions of yours before we have to get going again.' Flora looked expectantly at him.

'Just a few, then,' Gareth said.

'You first.' Trudy put her knife and fork together.

'OK. How about the time I locked myself in the conductor's office?'

'Are you serious?'

'Would I lie to you, Flora? In my defence, the locking mechanism was faulty.'

'What happened?'

'I got on the intercom to the driver and he sent his mate down the train to rescue me. I don't know how he managed it, but he let me out before we got to the next station. It was a near thing, though.'

'I can imagine. Trudy? Your turn to frighten me!'

'I still blush when I think of this one. It was when I was working on a train that had a first-class coach. The service was very crowded, and when we set off and I started checking tickets in the first-class section, I noticed this little — well, 'bag lady' is probably the most polite way of putting it.' Trudy paused. 'I can see you remember it, Gareth.'

'Oh, yes, we all fell about laughing when we heard.'

'Beware of company gossip, Flora. Well, I was still quite new and determined to get things right, but I certainly blew this one. I got closer to the bag lady, and there she was — her fur coat looked about a hundred years old! She had yards of scarf wound round her neck and a funny woollen hat pulled down over her eyebrows; finger-less gloves, carrier bags on the seat beside her, and one on the table with an old brown thermos flask sticking up from it. Goodness knows what other goodies were in there. So I asked, in my most polite voice, to see her ticket.'

'*Excuse me, madam*?' Gareth chimed in.

'Absolutely like that. Anyway, madam delved into a pocket in her tatty coat and produced a railway ticket and a railcard. She said, 'Here you are, my dear,' in a very posh voice, and at the time, I wondered if she'd genuinely mistaken the carriage for an ordinary one, or decided to try her luck as the rest of the train was so crowded. Anyway, when I glanced at her ticket it *was* a first-class one; but the real shock was the name on her railcard.'

'Please hurry up! The suspense is killing me,' Flora said.

Gareth chortled.

'I was within moments of asking Lady Emily Warburton to leave the first-class section! Can you imagine how stupid I felt?'

4

'Why did it have to happen to me? I know a little Spanish, so I asked them if they spoke the language, but all I got were blank looks!' Flora wailed into her mobile phone as she stood outside the driver's cabin, while the train got up speed and the countryside whizzed past the window.

'It's very unfortunate.' Trudy's voice filtered into her ear. 'But we're not allowed to let passengers travel without valid tickets. I blame those poor people's employers for dumping them at the station, knowing none of them speak English.'

'Oh, my goodness, it's just occurred to me,' Flora said. 'They're Polish. I'm sure they're Polish. I wonder if Roman's on the train.'

'Good thinking! He should be there as it's still term-time. Why not put out an announcement and ask him to come to the front? Knowing him, he'll be only too pleased to help.'

'OK. Thanks, Trudy. I'll text you later so you know what happened.'

Flora hurried off to make her request over the PA system. If necessary, she'd have to get one of the drivers to back her up by requesting the four passengers who'd been so badly let down by their employer to get off the train. She'd taken out her mobile phone and, by means of signs, tried to make them understand that they should contact someone who spoke English so she could ask where the men were intending to travel, and also explain to them how much money they needed to pay.

She progressed down the carriage, issuing tickets and hoping to see Roman appear. To her relief, the tall teenager came through the sliding doors and loped down the aisle towards her.

'Roman, thank you so much! I need you to translate for me, please.'

'Yeah? Polish or French?'

'Polish, please! Don't show off,' she teased. Knowing those poor people could now have help from someone who spoke their language gave her a great feeling of relief.

'Is it the four guys sitting halfway down this carriage?'

'That's the ones. They can't speak English, but one kept showing me tickets that were out of date.'

'Let's see if I can help.' Roman strode down the aisle, Flora following him, feeling rather like a mother hen watching over her chick.

Whatever Roman said to the group prompted a discussion between him and one of the men. It didn't take long for the student to find out what had happened.

He turned to Flora, a serious look upon his face. 'They've been duped. They were dropped off at the station this morning, given those useless tickets, and told to get on the first train that came in. They've been labouring at

41

a local building site and were promised more work in a different place. But they need to clock on there before they get any money for the work they've already done.' He raised his eyebrows. 'Sounds decidedly dodgy to me, Flora. They assumed their tickets were good.'

'Do the men have money to pay for new ones?'

'Yes.' Roman hesitated. 'They need to get off at Pennock, so let me know how much that costs for four people, and I'll help them sort out the cash. I hope the person picking them up is on the level and treats them well.'

'Me too! Roman, thank you so much.'

'You're welcome.'

She assured him she'd make sure the Poles left the train at the correct station, and for the rest of the journey, she was kept busy, though she still felt cross at the thought of people being exploited. Maybe there had been some sort of misunderstanding, but she doubted she would ever know how the men got on. Despite it being so early in her railway career, she knew the daily passenger load varied, and you could never rely on meeting someone again.

On arrival at Cardiff, Flora headed for the mess room, looking forward to a sit down and something to eat and drink. But as she made her way towards the stack of trays, she could hear a buzz of conversation and tittering that seemed to begin as soon as she closed the door behind her and headed for the buffet counter.

Someone came up behind her, just as she was panicking that a notice had been attached to her back or she had a smut on her nose.

'Well, well, if it isn't Flora, our famous train conductor!'

She whirled round and came face to face with Gareth.

'Remember me?'

'Who could ever forget you?'

His face creased in a grin. 'I hear you've had an eventful morning.'

'You mean those Polish workers?

How on earth did you hear about that?'

He gestured to the assistant. 'Shall we order our food?'

Puzzled, Flora gave her order and moved towards the drinks machines, closely followed by Gareth.

'Would you like company? It seems you don't know what a celebrity you are.'

'Celebrity? You're having a laugh! Let's share a table and you can tell me what's going on.' Flora waited for the dispenser to fill her mug with frothy white coffee.

Gareth collected his drink and led the way to a table for two in a corner. Flora decided to ignore all the curious glances and smirks from the mostly male railway employees and sat down opposite him.

'Come on, then. Tell me how you know about something that happened barely two hours ago.'

'It seems someone on your train heard you trying to get through to the Polish guys and then saw you come back with the young man who could speak their language.' He stirred sugar into his tea. 'Thanks to the joys of social media, you've 'gone viral', as they say.'

'No! That's awful, Gareth. Have people got nothing better to do?'

'Apparently people are saying it's good publicity for the rail company. How you used your initiative and saved the day.'

At once Flora could hear Mr Gorgeous in her head, telling her she'd saved the day by finding the missing teddy bear. How embarrassing was today's episode, though?

'Don't look so worried,' said Gareth. 'Here comes our food, by the way.'

Flora thanked the assistant. 'I had to ring Trudy for advice. I just couldn't bear the thought of having to throw those men off the train.'

'The mind boggles,' said Gareth. 'I wouldn't be surprised to find the local radio stations pick up on this. It reflects well on you and the company. What's more, I'll be able to tell my mates I had lunch with you today.' He gave her a very warm smile and seemed about to say something else, but Flora thought he must have thought better of it.

'I don't want to see any of the posts or tweets,' she said firmly. 'I'm still new at this job, and I can do without distractions.'

Gareth stared at her. 'You're an unusual girl. I thought I'd better check whether you knew what was happening.'

'It doesn't take long, does it? For people to spread the word, I mean.'

'It's phenomenal, but don't worry, it'll probably fizzle out as quickly as it began. You should be prepared for passengers to stare at you, though. Mind you,' he said, 'I wouldn't mind betting you get plenty of that already.'

Flora treated him to a very hard stare. Sometimes she wished she lived in a world where people still telephoned each other at home, and sat down with pen and paper to write long letters to their friends and family.

* * *

Jack Slater flew through the revolving door of the foyer and set off down the street. A last-minute phone call had detained him at the office, but he might still make the next westbound train if he was lucky. Otherwise, he'd be cooling his heels on the platform until the next one, meaning he'd be late for supper — and, more importantly, Ellie's bath time and bedtime story.

He reached the station and made a beeline for the steps up to the covered bridge across the railway tracks. He knew his train was standing at the platform, but would he get down to the other side in time? Jack clattered down the steps and across the platform just as the train conductor hopped back on board and closed the door behind her. This was a minor station and there was no train dispatcher.

'Please?' he shouted, as he lunged towards the door handle. 'Can I get on?'

The door opened and Jack fell into the train.

'Are you alright, sir?' The conductor sounded a little disapproving.

Jack sucked in air. 'Phew. Yeah, I'm still in one piece, but I'm sorry about the last-minute dash.'

Finally he realised who he was standing next to. 'It's you, isn't it? You're the girl who rescued my daughter's teddy bear! You look so different in uniform. I saw you on the train one day last week, and — and — ' He tailed off, horrified at how narrowly he'd avoided blurting out how much he'd wanted to speak to her and how pleased he was to see her again. She must be fed up to the back teeth with male passengers coming on to her, hoping to chat her up.

'I'm pleased to have been able to help.' She had such a lovely smile. Such a silky voice. In fact, everything about her seemed lovely. 'Now, if you'd like to take a seat, I must get on . . . '

'Of course.' Jack set off down the

carriage and found a seat. The train was pretty crowded, but he wouldn't be late home now and he'd be able to tell Ellie he'd met the lady who was sitting near them on the train that day they took Freddie Bear to the wildlife park.

He didn't attempt to make conversation when Flora — this time he'd read her name badge — checked his ticket. She wore no rings, but someone so pretty was bound to have a boyfriend. Anyway, Jack reckoned he must be at least eight years her senior. Why was he thinking like this?

He gazed out at the ancient ruined castle he must have passed dozens and dozens of times without ever bothering to check its name. He watched a tractor trundling across a field towards a grey stone farmhouse, and wondered if the driver was the farmer returning to his wife for tea and a chat before going back out to check on his stock at the end of his day. A pang of envy hit him, and all of a sudden he felt a wave of loneliness. He was wishing for something lost — something precious that he probably wouldn't ever know again. That was a silly thing to dwell on, though, wasn't it? He had a six-year-old daughter and a demanding job, not forgetting the house-hunting project, to keep him more than occupied. Romance, or the pursuit of it, was one too many thing to think about.

5

Some days Flora happened to see the man she privately called Mr Gorgeous, and some days she didn't. She'd seen him board the train at Glanalan, and he must work in Wolf's Hill; but with her varying shift patterns, she sometimes missed his comings and goings. Now and then they exchanged a greeting or even a few words, generally about the weather — or on one occasion, his small daughter's progress at school, when Flora had plucked up courage to enquire about Ellie.

Mr Gorgeous, beaming at her, said Ellie had two special friends, and also that she thought the world of her teacher. 'Such a relief,' he'd said.

Flora, of course, wondered what might have been going on in the child's life to cause her dad to worry, which he obviously had been doing. But there was never sufficient time to hold a long conversation. Until one morning, when the service was disrupted by something totally unscheduled.

Kevin, who was driving the train, buzzed for her to go and see him shortly after the service left Glanalan. Flora, who had noticed how the train was crawling along the track rather than picking up speed, hurried to the front, by which time they were at a standstill. Kevin's co-driver, Bryn, let her into the cab.

'Guess what — we have cattle on the line!'

'Oh, what a nuisance.' Flora bit her lip. 'I hope the animals aren't in danger.'

'Nothing reported,' Kevin said. 'But it's taking a while to round them up, and I'm afraid we have to sit here until we're given the go-ahead to continue to Redbush.'

'Do you want me to make the announcement?' Flora asked.

'No, you're all right. I'll do it, but you can bet some people won't hear and you'll be asked what's going on.'

'This is where your powers of tact and diplomacy will be called upon,' Bryn said, giving her a smile. 'As soon as we hear something, we'll let everyone know via the PA system.'

Flora left them to it. The refreshment trolley operator was making her way along the aisle. Flora whispered to her that their driver was about to announce the delay, and no one knew quite how long it would be before they could set off again.

She noticed Mr Gorgeous sitting near the rear of the coach, and made her way slowly towards him after the driver came on the PA to inform the passengers of the delay and the reason for it.

Jack looked up as she reached his seat. 'Morning, Flora. I've heard of leaves on the line, but I gather we have cattle holding us up today!'

'I'm afraid so.' She hesitated. 'I hope this won't cause a long delay, but of course it's totally out of our hands.'

'Maybe you should ask whether there's a cow whisperer on board?'

'If there is, let's hope he doesn't mind sprinting up the track! I sometimes wonder, if I could ask all my passengers what they did for a living or what kind of life they'd had, it'd be absolutely fascinating.'

Jack nodded. 'While I think of it, I heard about you and the Polish guys.' He made a face. 'I'm pretty hopeless with social media, but people at the office were talking about it.'

Flora nodded. 'That makes two of us where social media's concerned. Goodness, it was a storm in a teacup, really. I felt so sorry for those men, being left in such a position. It was such a relief having someone on board who could actually talk to them so we knew what was going on.'

'You mean the tall young man with the fair hair?' Jack raised his eyebrows. 'He and I have a discussion sometimes, though we're not on the train together for long. He's a lovely young man with an enquiring mind. Tells me he's off to Poland for the summer, then back to do his last year at Sixth Form College.'

'Yes, Roman's a lovely boy.' She liked the fact that Mr Gorgeous considered himself to be rubbish at the whole social media thing, but all of a sudden she felt tongue-tied. He was looking up at her with those fabulous eyes of his, and all she could do was conjure up a weak smile. What was she like!

'Ships that pass in the night,' he said. 'Not a very realistic summing-up, but you know what I mean.'

'I do,' she said. 'Some passengers travel on a Wednesday, for example, probably going to the market at Parkswell; and a few, like Roman, catch the same time train each way, Monday to Friday.'

'My schedule's a bit unpredictable,' Jack said. 'Usually I take the train for my office days and work from home on the others. It's very different from when I used to commute in and out of London.'

Flora waited for more, but he dropped his gaze and she noticed his jaw tighten. It was as if he'd reminded himself of something from his past and wished he hadn't done so. Maybe he was regretting getting into conversation with her.

She cast around for something intelligent to say, and failed miserably. 'I suppose I have a mobile workplace! To be honest, since I started this job I sometimes dream about trains. You'd think my poor brain would've had enough of them in the daytime without conjuring up weird situations while I'm asleep.'

He nodded. She could have kicked herself. He must be bored to tears with her chattering on. And whatever had possessed her to speak about dreaming? She'd even had a dream about Mr Gorgeous himself the other night. He'd been driving the train she was working on, and she'd spent time sitting in the cab beside him, while the train made its way through what looked like a dense forest, full of little creatures jumping around and shinning up tree trunks. What had all that been about?

'I hope this won't make you too late for work,' she said, moving off.

'Thanks.' He was taking out his laptop. Probably he was relieved to be rid of her.

★　★　★

Jack waited for his laptop to respond. If there was a delay, he might as well work on the proposal he was preparing. Hopefully that would help him stop fantasising about Flora. She was so different from Ellie's mum, having light brown hair, and being of a taller and slightly slimmer build. But, apart from her low, husky voice, it was her smile that got to him. The smile which lit up her face and which so appealed to him — although, that first time they met, when he'd seen her as just another passenger, he hadn't taken much notice of her. But he'd had Ellie with him on that occasion, seizing all his attention.

Now, every time he stood on the platform waiting for his train to arrive, he wondered whether Flora would be on board. It seemed an odd job for her to be doing. She looked so young. He longed to know the story behind her career choice, but she probably regarded him as another boring businessman. Anyway, did he really want to begin all that dating hassle again? One or two friends had gently suggested he might try an online dating service, but the thought of using the Internet to meet someone didn't appeal in any way. In fact, the prospect terrified him.

He'd met his late wife when they'd worked for the same company near London, as part of a team involved with a regeneration project. More than one person had told him he was too young to settle down, but he'd ignored the advice; and when Ellie came along, he was twenty-six years of age and thrilled at the prospect of becoming a dad. Fate, in the form of a serious traffic accident, had torn his adored wife from them, and put a stop to any thoughts of a sister or brother for his daughter.

Again, everyone knew better than him. Everyone reassured him he was still so young, he had plenty of time to meet someone else and marry again. Why people couldn't just mind their own business, he'd never know. He understood that they meant well, but he wasn't outgoing like some of his colleagues were.

He'd been thinking of Flora on and off for some weeks now, a situation that intrigued and at the same time bothered him. He was well aware he'd gone through a long grieving process and needed to move on. He was also well aware it would do him good to find a girlfriend instead of spending all his leisure time with his family. But poor little motherless Ellie — what sort of a dad would he be if he didn't try to spend as much time as possible with her?

Jack's mind wasn't on his work. He

always found it easier to concentrate when sitting at his desk, whether in the office or in a corner of his bedroom in the place he currently called home. He needed to crack on with finding a house, having sold the one in mid-Wales almost a year ago. Where had all that time gone since the move from London? Finding a place somewhere not too distant from Ellie's grandparents would be practical, as he'd also have his sister-in-law and family within an easy drive. Ellie's aunt was very happy to look after her niece whenever Jack needed childcare, as her own daughter was only a year older than his, and the two girls played well together.

Jack abandoned his current project until later, and opened up an estate agent's website to check on properties in his price range. Two looked promising, so he bookmarked them. It would be sensible to sort out the house situation soon, though life would become a little more complicated once he no longer lived under his in-laws' roof. But Ellie was growing fast, and while he valued the cosseting she received from her loving family, he knew she also needed to learn independence. Fortunately, she was a confident little girl; lately, he'd noticed her paying much less attention to Freddie the bear, and becoming more interested in girly things.

If only his daughter hadn't got it in her head that he ought to find her a mummy. The new friends she'd made at Ashfield Primary all had mummies. So why couldn't she?

Jack sighed. No pressure there, then.

* * *

Flora breathed a sigh of relief as the driver announcement came over the public address system. She'd felt a little under pressure as some passengers decided to confide their problems in her. One man had a hospital appointment in Parkswell and was worried about having to turn up late for it. Two young mums were off to Cardiff for a spa day and posh afternoon tea — with a glass of bubbly to look forward to! They'd got their childcare arrangements sorted and were disappointed by the prospect of having to cut short their treat. Flora tried her best to remain positive and sympathise with her passengers, all the while longing to hear that the cows had been corralled — or whatever the expression was — and the train could continue its journey.

She checked her watch. They were twenty minutes behind schedule, and there was a limit to how much speed Driver Kev could achieve. One of the passengers was in a wheelchair, and Flora needed to be on hand to get the ramp in position ready for the lady, who'd be leaving the train at the next halt.

Flora looked through the window and noticed they were passing a primary school. Some children were playing a game of rounders, having plenty of fun and exercise in the fresh air. A little group of onlookers sitting on the grass looked round at the sound of the train rumbling down the track, and began waving furiously. Flora chuckled as several passengers joined in, and she too gave the pupils a wave as she moved towards the wheelchair user, deciding she'd ask if she was the lady Trudy had mentioned.

'I'm so sorry you've been delayed.'

'Time and cows wait for no man,' said the passenger, eyeing Flora up and down. 'Haven't seen you before today. Are you new? Do you happen to know my friend Trudy?'

'Yes, I'm still quite new. If it hadn't been for Trudy, I'd probably have been thrown out before now! I'm Flora, and I think you must be Serena. She told me to look out for the lady who always wears lovely bright clothes.'

Serena smiled. 'That's typical of Trudy. Most people see the wheelchair, not the person.'

Flora didn't quite know how to reply to that.

'It's all right, my dear. Fortunately,

not everyone's the same.'

'Trudy told me you enjoy driving as well as travelling by train.'

'That's right. My car's being serviced, and today was the earliest they could fit it in. I decided, rather than put off visiting my oldest friend, I'd take the train. I rang her so she knew not to set off too soon to meet me.'

'Well, I hope you have a lovely day together. I'll be with you in a minute, Serena.'

'I usually wait until other people have got off, my dear.'

'We're not very busy today, but I'll get the ramp organised; and if anyone's desperate to get off quickly, they can go along to the next door. No worries.'

But the procedure Flora had practised in training wasn't working out for her, and she was having difficulty securing the ramp. She looked around in desperation. How cringe-making it would be to have to put in a call to one of the drivers to come and help her, a mere woman!

'Can I be of help?'

Flora looked up into the blue, blue eyes of Mr Gorgeous. 'Yes, please,' she replied. Did her heart truly skip a beat? 'If you could step on to the platform and see what's preventing the ramp from settling into position, it would be really helpful.'

'OK.' Jack got out of the train and stooped to examine the ramp.

'Any luck?' Flora was conscious of time ticking by.

'I think you have the ramp in the right position, but something's stopping it from clicking into place.' He straightened up. 'If the lady steers her chair to the doorway and you keep hold of the handles, I can guide her safely down.'

Flora looked anxiously at him. Mr Gorgeous was by no means a strapping great hunk. He was of slim build, though probably not far off six feet tall.

'Are you sure? I can get one of the drivers to help if you prefer. I'd hate you to strain your back.'

'Make sure the lady's happy to trust

herself to me, and let's go for it. I'm stronger than I look!'

Flora, who'd been telling herself she'd given up blushing, felt heat flood her cheeks. Was Mr Gorgeous a mind-reader?

Her passenger wheeled herself forward. 'I'll make sure to keep the brakes partly on,' she said.

Flora guided the chair forward, and Mr Gorgeous made sure of a safe landing. A woman walked along the platform, obviously come to meet her friend Serena, and Jack lifted the ramp up and pushed it back onto the train before boarding.

'Got it,' Flora said. 'Thank you very much indeed. I was dreading the guys making jokes about this job not being suitable for a woman in a man's world!'

Flora did what she had to do, and the train began sliding away from the platform. Her knight in shining armour stood, facing her, in the section between two carriages. For moments he and she gazed at each other, swaying to the train's motion.

'Do you have much of that sort of thing to put up with? Teasing, I mean. I do hope not.' His expression was serious.

'Now and then I get ribbed, but I try to give as good as I get.'

The train was picking up speed. Flora needed to get on with checking that the passengers who'd just boarded all possessed tickets. Suddenly, she was thrown forwards against her companion's chest. Swiftly, he encircled her with his arms, steadying her. For a moment, she felt as though her heart beat to the same rhythm as his.

Flora looked into those cornflower-blue eyes, and was struck by the strangest sensation. Could he possibly feel the same connection as she did? If only he did, that would be a dream come true. For one startling second, she wondered if he was going to kiss her.

6

'Whoops!' Flora's Mr Gorgeous released her as the train stopped lurching and resumed its steady progress.

'Sorry,' she said. 'You'd think I could stand on my own two feet by now. I hope I haven't lost my sea legs.' She also hoped her voice didn't sound as wobbly to him as it did to her.

'We can all get knocked off course sometimes,' he said, holding her gaze.

If he only knew how right he was! 'Well, I must get on,' she said. 'Thanks again for all your help back there.'

He shrugged. 'No problem. You were doing fine, Flora. A lot of things are easier with an extra pair of hands.'

They were looking at each other again. But if her suspicion about his feelings had been accurate, wouldn't this be the perfect moment for him to make a move? Ask her when her next day off was, perhaps? At least tell her his name, given he had the advantage of knowing hers. Was it Adam, Ben, or Charles? She'd trawled through the whole alphabet, trying to decide which name he best suited, and she still hadn't a clue what he was called. He didn't use a season ticket because he didn't travel regularly enough. Anyway, hadn't she decided he must be a married man? If that assumption proved to be right, as she knew deep down it must, to ask her out would be taboo.

Flora smiled and went on her way. Everything was as it should be — except, of course, that the service was running late, and that would cut down her time at Parkswell, where she planned to grab a bite to eat and have a gossip with Trudy. Whatever magic had shimmered in the air moments earlier had disappeared like Cinderella's sequins at midnight.

★　★　★

'Hi!' Flora waved at Trudy and made her way across the restaurant.

Trudy tapped her wrist. 'What sort of time d'you call this?' Her eyes sparkled with fun.

'If I say *cattle on the line*, does that explain? Oh, you star, you've got me a coffee.'

'I heard the announcement that your train was approaching. I also ordered you a big breakfast, to save time. I hope that's all right.'

'Perfect, thanks.' Flora hesitated. 'It was quite an eventful sector, that last one.'

'You haven't gone viral again, have you? I can't believe how many people were talking about you that time.'

'Ha ha, very funny. Don't remind me! I knew nothing until I happened to meet Gareth in here and he told me what was going on.'

'Well, you dealt with the situation brilliantly, and in the best possible way for those Polish guys.'

'It helped, having you on the other

end of the phone. I had a lovely email from management, thanking me for using my initiative. Dad told me one of the Welsh newspapers tracked down the men and made sure they were being treated properly at their new building site.'

'That's good to hear.' Trudy looked up. 'Here's our food.'

'I must keep an eye on the clock.'

'Me too. My train's due out before yours. But while I've got you here, I'd like to invite you to a party.'

Already Flora was attacking her plateful of egg, bacon and sausage. 'Is this a works thing?'

'No, it's a private party to celebrate my husband and me reaching our tenth wedding anniversary. It's a long way ahead, but I need to give friends who work for the rail company plenty of time so they can request not to be put on the roster on the day of the party. It's only three or four of you, but I'd love you all to be there.'

'Thank you very much. It sounds lovely, but — '

'But what?' Trudy picked up her coffee mug and sipped the hot liquid.

'I'm not very good at parties. I — I never know anything about the latest music or what's showing at the local cinema.'

'There's only one of those within reasonable distance of us!' Trudy grinned. 'Anyway, do go on. I'm finding this fascinating.'

'I can't think why. I still keep up with fashion — it's kind of a habit since working all those years in the shop. But I enjoy watching old black-and-white films and listening to the kind of music my gran enjoys.' Flora picked up her slice of toast. 'Um, I watch cricket when I can, and — there, I knew it! You're laughing at me already.'

'In a good way.' Trudy leaned forward. 'Is there anything else you'd like to share?' Her eyes twinkled. 'Hearing you talk like this reminds me of something I've heard about a person my husband mentions now and then.'

'Does that mean there's someone else like me around? I prefer reading real books, and I hate online shopping. I like to have a real theatre ticket, not a printout on white paper. My dad says I'm a seventy-three-year-old in the body of a twenty-three-year-old!'

'Love it! I've never noticed, but do you have a smartphone, apart from your company one?'

'I don't. My personal phone is for making calls and texting. That's why I hadn't a clue I was being talked about on the Internet until Gareth told me.'

'There are plenty of people who think like you, Flora, though admittedly not so many of them in their early twenties.' Trudy scooped up some baked beans and paused. 'I know what was niggling at me. My husband has a friend who you'd probably get on with, because it sounds like he feels very much as you do. The ironic thing is, he has to use the latest technology in his job, but apparently his phone is only one step up from the ones that used to be the size of a brick.'

'Come on!'

'OK, I guess Dan — that's my husband — was exaggerating, but you get the picture?'

'All I can say is, this friend of Dan's sounds nice.'

'Well, hopefully, if he and you can both make it, you'll meet one another at our party. Dan works in the same building as Jack Slater does, though they're in different departments. They got friendly because they both like cricket, and they put together a local authority team sometimes.'

'So I might have someone to talk to who doesn't think I'm odd, then? What's the date of your party?'

'It's the last Saturday in August. We'll be sending invitations out, but I'm letting everyone know the date upfront.'

'Is your husband's friend definitely coming, do you know?'

'He's not sure at the moment. Jack's

a widower, and he's currently looking to buy a house somewhere reasonably close to family. I think Dan has him down as a maybe. Jack also has a little daughter, so she's a big priority for him, as you can imagine.'

'That little girl must miss her mum. How sad for them.'

'Yes, indeed. I gather the child was only toddling when Jack's wife was killed in a car accident, so she doesn't remember her mum.'

'It can't be easy for a man, bringing up a daughter on his own.'

'He's a bit touchy on that subject, according to Dan. Jack moved to Pembrokeshire from mid-Wales for two reasons. One was to stop people from trying to marry him off; and, more importantly, the other was to be nearer his wife's family.'

'That sounds sensible.'

'Oh, this guy's very sensible, or so I'm told. I don't actually know him, though he uses the train when he has to work at Wolf's Hill.'

'Wouldn't it be odd if you'd already met him without realising he was your husband's colleague?'

'I suppose it would, but I doubt I'll meet him now I'm working a different route. And he may not even have known my name until he and Dan got to know each other better. You know what men can be like.' She put her knife and fork together. 'Speaking of different routes, it's time for me to love you and leave you.'

'Great to see you, Trudy! My turn to buy lunch next time, and I'll put that date in my diary.'

'Not in your phone, Flora?'

'That'd be a first, wouldn't it?'

*   *   *

To Flora's relief, the westbound service proved to be much more peaceful than that morning's eastbound one. The best thing was, she met someone who, again, Trudy had mentioned to her.

The passenger, who had raven black

hair and was unusually tall for a Welsh woman, boarded the train at Redbush along with several others. Flora knew it was market day in the town, and this contributed to more people using the train on a Thursday than any other day of the week.

Flora made her way down the train, eventually meeting up with the dark-haired woman in the last coach. She wore an eye-catching knitted coat in a beautiful shade of deep charcoal, with a deep pink scarf wound around her neck.

'I haven't seen the other conductor for ages. Trudy, I mean.' The passenger held out her ticket for Flora to check.

'She used to be a regular on this route, but she's working another one for the time being.'

'Do give her my best if you meet up with her.'

'Are you Bethan, by any chance?'

The woman smiled. 'That's me. What has Trudy been saying about me? Nothing terrible, I hope.'

'Of course not! I wondered, seeing your beautiful woollen coat, if it was you she'd mentioned. She told me about the amazing things you make.'

Bethan stretched out her arm so Flora could touch the material. 'This coat's made from alpaca wool. You can feel how soft it is. Although it's finer than sheep's wool, it's actually warmer. I set off very early on market days and need to bundle up in my woollies, even in late spring.'

'I know what you mean. Are those llamas I've noticed in the field further along this route?' Flora asked. 'Or are they alpacas? I've often wondered and never found out.'

'Do you mean the flock we can see just outside of St Katherine?'

'I think so. They're quite big animals, aren't they?'

'They are, and those are llamas. Alpacas are smaller. I keep a small flock of sheep, but a friend gave me this yarn, knowing I'd make good use of it.'

'You must be very talented to be able

to make all those lovely knitted garments.'

'I don't know about that, but I enjoy what I do. I have a website, and that keeps me busy too.'

'I bet it does.' Flora looked down the carriage. 'There are a couple of youngsters at the other end being silly. I'd better go and have a word.'

'Yes, tell them someone has complained about the noise they're making.'

Flora grinned. 'I'll put my stern face on.'

'Do you enjoy your job? Apart from passengers behaving badly, I mean.'

'Yes,' she answered without hesitation. 'I really do.'

7

Flora could hardly wait for her two days off in a row. The following Friday, she planned to visit Marion. They'd drive to Parkswell from her aunt's house and look around the shops. Flora was keen to buy a new dress as a result of the party invitation from Trudy and her husband.

A party! The prospect excited her as much as it terrified her. Her ex-boyfriend had disliked parties — disliked lots of things, come to think of it. So their outings together had mostly consisted of visits to the pub, sometimes playing skittles with his farming friends. Flora had been too good at skittles. A lucky beginner, Tom called her! She could tell he didn't enjoy it if she hit all the pins down in one strike.

Sometimes she wondered what might have happened if she hadn't taken up her new job. Tom hadn't approved of that either. When she told him about her training course, he'd said it might be nice if she moved into the farmhouse with him. One day, his parents would move into the new bungalow planned on the other side of the yard, and he'd need someone to keep him company in the farmhouse.

What kind of message did that send? It was at that moment Flora knew exactly where she stood. He might or might not decide he wanted her to become his wife. He'd probably go for the conventional option, but she knew how foolish she would be to agree.

'It's for the best, Tom,' she'd told him, a few days before beginning her new life.

Of course, he hadn't agreed, and promptly asked why she hadn't con- sulted him sooner regarding her plans. She'd shaken her head sadly. He'd driven her home in silence, seemingly unable to find it within him to wish her luck with her new career.

Now her days were chock-a-block with funny, frustrating, unexpected events involving the many passengers who got on and off her train for such a variety of reasons.

* * *

Flora looked at her watch as she waited to board the train. It should be along any moment now. She stood on her own at the far end of the platform, hoping nobody would recognise her and maybe want to chat. Much longer, and someone would probably ring the men manning the signal box back down the line to see where the train had got to.

All of a sudden she heard a little cheer from a group of people waiting a few yards further up from her. The train had appeared in the distance. When it came to a halt, Flora pushed the door release and jumped inside, sitting down in the first free double seat she saw in the last carriage. She hadn't even looked to see if she knew today's train conductor, because he or she would be along soon to check tickets.

When the male conductor stopped beside her, she looked up and smiled, offering her staff pass. 'Good morning.'

'Hi,' he said, checking her name. 'Oh, so you're Flora?' He chuckled. 'Or, should I say, the famous Flora?'

'Shush, please! I'm trying to make myself invisible. It's my day off.'

'I don't blame you,' said her colleague. 'But why the busman's holiday, if you'll pardon the expression?'

'I'm off to see my aunt. She lives at Bell's Hill, so we're going to drive to the shopping mall for a few hours. She likes to go by car in case she gets tired and wants to set off home.'

He screwed up his face. 'Shopping? Rather you than me. Anyway, enjoy your day off.' He moved on down the carriage.

Flora pulled a freebie paper from the pocket of the seatback in front and began reading. Thankfully, no one she recognised was sitting anywhere nearby, and with luck she could leave the train as unobtrusively as she'd boarded it.

She turned to the astrology section and checked out her star sign.

With a powerful, bright force of energy driving you today, you're bound to attract more attention than usual — so don't you dare be shy! Everyone you'll encounter is in an unusually receptive frame of mind, so it's a great day to make new friends or romantic conquests.

Flora stared at the newsprint in disbelief. She didn't usually bother reading these forecasts, and surely this one proved how right she was not to do so. There was no way she'd be attracting attention, travelling incognito on the train, and about to go wandering around a Welsh market town with her elderly aunt. What rubbish!

She turned to the puzzles section and began looking at the crossword clues. This made her recollect the conversation she'd had with Trudy over lunch not long ago. She'd forgotten to mention how much she enjoyed doing crosswords and codewords. Opening her handbag to find a pen, she wondered whether this might be a pastime she shared with the man Trudy's husband played cricket with. It would be fun to get to know someone who was a bit of a Luddite like she was. But if he didn't happen to feel as strongly about the onslaught of modern technology as she did, would he think she was too old-fashioned to make good girlfriend material?

She was jumping ahead and being unrealistic. Trudy knew hardly anything about her husband's friend, except that he was a single dad. Maybe it was safer to fantasise about Mr Gorgeous, and try not to dwell on a stranger who might not even turn up when the night of the anniversary party arrived.

* * *

Jack sat back in his seat and gazed out at the changing landscape. He'd been

85

reading through notes he'd made for an upcoming presentation and printed off the evening before. He knew he was far more likely to spot errors when reading a paper document rather than one viewed onscreen. So what if people teased him? He was used to it. Sometimes he wondered, if all the computers linked to the office system stopped working, resulting in a technical blackout, how everyone would cope. It was a sobering thought, and one many people probably never even considered. His daughter had never known a world without computers and nor had he, he reminded himself. But when he was a child there hadn't been such a flood of electronic goods on the market. He'd laughed out loud when Ellie asked if she could have an iPad, but her teacher assured him that this request was perfectly normal.

Deep in thought, he barely noticed the passengers waiting to board at the next stop. But, on her own, down the end of the platform, he caught a glimpse of a young woman who he was sure was Flora, unless he was hallucinating. He thought twice about wandering down the train to check if he was right. But she wasn't in uniform and would probably not welcome him intruding upon her space.

They were well away from the last station, passing a rambling old house, its grey stone walls warmed by the sunshine and its back turned to the railway line. Jack noticed three pairs of green Wellington boots standing like sentries outside the back door, plus a bicycle propped up against a garden shed. That made sense because he felt sure this was a family kind of house.

One of the sets of boots was made for a child's feet. The others obviously belonged to adults. He imagined the family: mum, dad and child. Maybe there was another baby on the way, or already here but not yet ready to pull on wellies with the rest of the family. Of course, he was brooding again, and needed to pull himself together.

Pack it in, Jack!

Soon the train would be arriving at Redbush, which meant he'd be getting off at the next stop, ready for another day at the office. He hadn't seen Flora working over the last few days. It might be that she was travelling to and fro at different times from him. He longed to approach her — but only if he could think of what to say to her without sounding like a stalker. *You've been on my mind a lot?* No way!

How embarrassing it would be if he asked her to go out with him and she turned him down. It would make life complicated when they saw each other in future, as he always bought his day return ticket on the train, with no one manning an office at his home station.

He sighed. Trust him to fall for someone whose job involved so many departures and arrivals. Even if she agreed to meet him, maybe just for a coffee to see how they got on, they'd probably find it difficult to decide whereabouts the date could happen.

Jack was so busy contemplating this problem he didn't notice the train slowing to a halt. And outside the windows on either side of the carriage, there was nothing but green fields. What on earth was happening now?

★   ★   ★

Just her luck! Flora knew something untoward must have happened for the driver to stop the train in the middle of nowhere. Was it more cattle on the line? Or would it be something more complicated? Passengers on this route mostly maintained a very happy-go-lucky attitude to short delays. In the winter, with low temperatures resulting in frozen points and sometimes dense fog, delays were inevitable. Today, with a blue sky and sunshine bathing the countryside, if the cows weren't to blame, maybe the delay was due to an engine fault or some electrical blip. Now she knew what it was like to sit there waiting for an announcement and wondering what the driver knew that the passengers didn't.

'Ladies and gentlemen, this is your driver speaking. I'd like to apologise for the unscheduled stop. This is due to a fault with the engine, and I'm afraid we'll have to stay here until assistance arrives.'

Flora could hear mutterings from some of her fellow passengers, but she concentrated on listening to the driver — who she recognised as Kevin, whose crew she'd been part of on the day of the Polish incident.

'Rest assured, we'll do our best to keep you comfortable during the wait,' the driver told them. 'The trolley will be coming your way soon, and complimentary drinks, including water, will be offered. As soon as I hear what's been decided, I shall of course inform you. Thank you for your patience.'

Now the muttering became a buzz. Flora put down the paper and reached in her jacket pocket for her phone. Her aunt wouldn't have left for the station yet, so she could ring to warn her about this interruption to their plans.

She was replacing her phone when she became aware of someone standing beside her.

'Hello, Flora. I thought it was you waiting on the platform back there. Haven't seen you for a while.'

8

Her throat dried. There was Mr Gorgeous smiling down at her — and here she was, gazing up at him open-mouthed. Charming!

'I hope this won't be too long a delay,' he said. 'It must be annoying for you, if this is your day off.'

'I'm on my way to Bell's Hill.' Flora, willing her hands not to tremble, folded them in her lap. 'I've had to ask my aunt not to set off for the station to meet me until we know what's what.'

He nodded. 'I'm due at the office, so I've texted to tell them the train's delayed. To be fair, the service isn't usually too bad.'

'That's good to know.' She longed to ask him to sit down, but wasn't sure if she should.

'Um, do you mind if I join you?' Mr Gorgeous looked anxiously at her; and

Flora's heart, if it hadn't been trapped in her ribcage, would surely have performed a treble somersault.

'Please do.'

She was sitting at a table for four. He pushed up the arm of the seat nearest the aisle and moved over to the window so he faced her.

'How does it feel, being a passenger for a change?'

'A little weird.' She hesitated. 'I'm sorry, I don't think I know your name, do I?'

He stared at her. 'Oh heck, I suppose you don't. I'm Jack Slater.' He held out his hand. 'I just know you as Flora.'

'Oh, Jack really suits you!' She stared at him, horrified at having blurted out her thoughts.

He shrugged. 'Thank you . . . I think.'

Their eyes met and suddenly Flora relaxed. 'It's great to meet you properly, Jack Slater. My full name's Flora Petersen.'

She couldn't believe her Mr Gorgeous was actually the young widower

Trudy had mentioned. Jack was, possibly, every bit as reserved as she was by nature, unless she tried to be otherwise, like at work. The question was, should she reveal how Trudy had described Jack, or should she keep the information to herself?

He'd drawn down the corners of his mouth, and at once she was reminded of his daughter's expression that time her teddy bear went missing and turned up under Flora's seat. She didn't like to see him looking so despondent.

'It's typical of me, not to think of something so basic as telling you my name,' Jack said. 'I think I checked your staff badge the very first time we met.'

She raised her eyebrows and he groaned. 'I should say, the first time I saw you in uniform, though it took me a while to realise it was you because you looked so different.'

'That's OK,' she said. 'How's your little girl, by the way?'

His whole expression brightened. 'Doing very well, thank you. I'm hoping, when I find the right house for us, she won't have to move to a different school.'

Flora sought the right words. She didn't want to appear nosey, nor did she wish to seem indifferent. She knew Jack's status, but he wasn't aware she did.

He came to her rescue. 'Ellie's mother was killed in a car accident when our little girl hadn't even started school.'

He linked his hands together on the table between them. Flora yearned to reach out to him, but resisted the temptation. This wasn't easy, but she knew that if they were to establish any kind of relationship, they needed to proceed with caution. Or at least keep the stabilisers on, as Auntie Marion would say.

'It's difficult to find the words to tell you how sorry I am,' Flora said.

Jack looked her in the eye. 'I know it is. But I need to move on, if only for Ellie's sake. To be honest, I try not to broadcast the fact that I'm a widower. Some people assume I'm playing the sympathy card, and — ' He pulled a wry face. ' — I've come across the occasional lady who seems to think I'm fair game to move in on.'

Flora nodded. She had no intention of telling him how much he lived up to her nickname for him, but now was not the time to be coy.

'I think I should be honest with you and tell you that one of my colleagues is married to someone you work with.'

'Really? How the heck do you know that?'

'I made my first trips on this route with Trudy.'

Jack looked blank. 'Sorry?'

'Trudy's married to Dan. You're both cricketers.'

Realisation dawned on his face. 'Well, I'm blessed. Yes, Dan's a good lad. I don't think he ever told me his wife's name, though.'

The expression describing men as coming from Mars and women from

Venus flashed into Flora's mind, but as she was on her best behaviour, she batted it away.

'Trudy invited me to their anniversary party, and — ' She took a deep breath. ' — for various reasons, she thought you and I were similar kinds of people.'

'Oh, poor you!' Jack put on a concerned face.

'Actually, more like poor *you*!' Impulsively, she reached out her hand, only to find he got there before her. She felt lost for words. Would he now confide that he'd like to be her friend, but he'd got a secret crush at the office that not even Dan knew about?

'Would you like something to drink, sir? Flora?' The refreshment trolley operator smiled down at them.

Great, thought Flora. She had a horrible premonition that being caught holding hands with a passenger, even though she wasn't on duty, would make one more thing for the staff to gossip about. Except this time, she couldn't care less. Because Jack still kept her hand in his, and for the first time in her life, Flora knew what people meant when they talked about floating on a fluffy pink cloud.

Once the trolley operator moved on, leaving Jack and Flora alone again with their drinks on the table, he smiled at her and squeezed her fingers. 'I'd better let you enjoy your coffee.'

'In a moment. Please, Jack, I don't want you to think Trudy and I were discussing you. Remember, I didn't have a clue what your name was, so Jack Slater didn't connect with you at all, even when she mentioned your daughter. Can you believe I was so slow to cotton on?'

'You had no reason to know who Trudy was talking about. I've probably come across her on this route, but I've travelled with two or three different female train conductors over the last year or so. If I go to the party, I'm sure I'll recognise her.' He took a swallow of his coffee.

'I was planning to buy a new dress for it today, but my plans may have been turned upside-down.'

'I guess we might be stuck here for hours. Had you considered that possibility?'

She shook her head. 'The company policy is for us always to remain optimistic!'

He laughed. 'Fair enough. But I'm thanking my lucky stars you took this train today. If it hadn't been for the engine failure, we might've each gone our different ways without getting this chance to talk to each other.'

'I wondered if you were on board this morning but I couldn't think of any sensible reason to walk down the train and check.'

'So you thought about me, even though you weren't on duty?' Jack's eyes sparkled.

Her heart did the boompity-boom thing again. 'I'm sorry. Maybe I shouldn't have said that.'

'Please don't apologise.' He reached

for her hand again. 'Oh dear, I hope I'm not being too presumptuous.'

'You're not.' She knew she was going to blush and she wasn't wrong. 'I'm very pleased you came to talk to me, Mr — erm — Jack!'

But his expression became wary. 'You're a friendly sort of person, Flora. I wouldn't want you to feel sorry for me.'

'I don't. Obviously, what happened to Ellie's mum was too sad for words, but you've been given a precious gift in your daughter. I know things must've been tough, but I'm sure you're a great dad, and I know she has loving family around.'

'Yes, she has. We're both fortunate in that. But, Flora, what about you? Here I am, presuming you're single, yet I can't believe there's no handsome rugby player or farmer waiting to put a ring on your finger.'

This was no time to allow Tom to muddy the waters. 'I'm unattached, and at the moment still living at home with my mother and father.' She stopped, horrified. 'Oh, I didn't mean anything unseemly by that remark! I wasn't hinting at anything!'

'Flora,' Jack said, 'you are so refreshing. In some ways, you remind me of the heroine of a classic novel.'

'I wish I didn't blush.'

'I'm glad you do. It fits your personality.'

'So which character do I remind you of?'

'Ha! That'll teach me.' He sat back and gazed out at the field. 'Maybe Jo March from *Little Women?* I don't know if you were a tomboy as a child, but if I was casting her in a film, I think you'd look the part.'

'Jo was always my favourite character in that book. So, you've actually read the novel?' She couldn't hide her surprise.

'My mother hung on to all her childhood books, and I was a dreadful bookworm as a boy.' Jack grinned. 'Though don't you dare tell your friend

Trudy. It's a dead cert I'd never hear the end of it at cricket practice.'

He looked up as the public address system crackled to life. 'Here we go.'

* * *

'And what happened next, may I ask?' Aunt Marion, having met Flora off the train, had bustled her into the car and they were now nearing their destination.

Flora chuckled. 'We were told the replacement train was pulling up on the track ahead, and we'd be on board soon. It was such a relief to get on our way.'

Aunt Marion snorted. 'Pull the other one! It sounds as though you could have sat there for hours, gazing into each other's eyes and murmuring sweet nothings.'

'Auntie, that's just not true.' Flora turned her head to the window to hide the huge smile on her face.

'At least the fellow got as far as

asking you on a date. The way you were describing it, I wondered if we were heading for a cliffhanger.'

'I thought it was touch and go at times, but we got there in the end. I still can't believe it's happened.'

Aunt Marion drew up at the car park entrance. 'Hmm, it sounds as if this young man's as backward in coming forward as you are. Thank goodness he saw sense.'

'Don't forget Jack's had a difficult few years. It can't be easy for him, beginning a new relationship after all this time.'

'Quite. Just let me get us parked and we'll head for the shopping mall. If we have a late lunch, we'll miss the queue in that vegetarian café you like, but the food choice won't be so great.'

'I know,' said Flora dreamily. 'Lovely, isn't it?' She turned to her aunt. 'Sorry, I was daydreaming. What did you say?'

'I was talking about food. Come on! We're only about an hour behind schedule. Things could be very much worse.'

In fact, things couldn't be much better, thought Flora. She and Jack were going for a meal together next evening. He'd suggested a restaurant not far from where she lived and one they'd both visited and agreed they liked.

'Until today, we've spent too much time saying nothing,' he'd told her. 'And not enough time getting to know one another. We don't even need to do the getting-together-for-a-coffee thing, as we've already accomplished that, courtesy of the railway company.'

She hadn't argued. Now, the big question was: should she look for a dress from a former decade, or should she go contemporary? Her aunt adored touring the charity shops, and kept her eye open for anything she thought might suit Flora, but rarely did either of them come across anything suitable from the fifties and sixties.

'Shall we start here?' Aunt Marion

decided for her, stopping outside one of the smaller shops run by volunteers.

Flora followed her inside with no great hopes of finding something. Apart from her love of retro clothing, she liked to think she was recycling, and she mentioned this to her aunt.

'It's probably because you spent all those years selling up-to-the-minute clothes,' Aunt Marion said. 'Though to my way of thinking, you were always a rather quaint child.'

'Thanks for that!' But Flora grinned. 'I didn't much like plastic, I remember.'

'Concentrate!' Marion pointed to a small selection of garments at the end of a rack. 'Don't ignore those. One or two of the fabrics look stunning.'

Flora, not wishing to offend her aunt, turned round and gasped. 'Oh my goodness, you're not exaggerating!'

9

'What's this young lady called, Jack? Not that I'd know her, of course.'

'Her name's Flora Petersen.' He smiled at his mother-in-law. 'Don't ask me about her folks because I know very little about her background.'

He knew that wouldn't go down well. Nor could he believe he was confiding in his late wife's mother, talking to her about the girl he'd asked to go on a date with him. He wasn't disappointed. Sure enough, Megan Riley bit her lip.

'Please don't think I disapprove, Jack. As for your friend's background, you can hardly bombard someone with personal questions before asking them to go out with you.' She hesitated. 'I think you know Charlotte wouldn't have wanted you to stay single for evermore.'

He stared out at the fields beyond the

patio where he and Megan were enjoying a glass of wine. Robbie, his father-in-law, was watching one of his favourite wildlife programmes, his grand-daughter on his knee. Ellie's bedtime was a little more flexible on Friday and Saturday nights.

'Megan, I don't want you to think I'm trying to replace your daughter. For one thing, that'd be impossible; and for another, it wouldn't be fair to look for someone who I think might make a suitable mother for Ellie.'

'You come as a package,' Megan said cheerfully. 'Could I ask whether your friend knows you have a young child?'

'Of course. We have to begin as we mean to go on.' He smiled, picturing Flora's slim hand gripping Freddie and waving the bear in the air. 'As it happens, Flora has already met Ellie, though only fleetingly.'

'How come?'

'Earlier this summer, I took Ellie to that wildlife park that opened down Redbush way, remember?'

Megan sipped her wine. 'Yes, I do, but you didn't mention meeting a young lady.'

'There was nothing to say. Flora was a passenger on the train, and Ellie mislaid her teddy bear just as we were approaching our station. Luckily, Flora found him on the floor, much to Ellie's delight.'

'I can imagine. But I thought you said this young lady was a train conductor.'

'She is, though not at the time we first clapped eyes on one another. I didn't take much notice of her, to be honest, except that she had a lovely voice and nice smile. I reckon I was in a bit of a flap, trying not to leave anything behind; and, well, you know me and tickets.'

'You generally forget where you put them.'

'It used to wind Charlotte up something rotten! In the end, she always insisted on taking care of our documents if we were going away.'

'It's good you can talk about her, Jack.'

'I need to talk about her, for Ellie's sake as well as mine. And yours,' he added hastily.

'Do you mind if I say something?'

'It depends what it is, mother-in-law dear!'

Megan smiled. 'Unless you've been leading a double life without Robbie and me knowing, I think this is the first date you've arranged in a very long while.'

'I've been extremely cautious in that direction, as you well know.'

'I do know. And that makes me suspect this particular young lady might be someone special.' She held up her hand. 'You don't need to say anything. Your private life's your own, and I'm not about to give you advice. Before too long, you and Ellie will be leaving us; and you'll need to make new friends, increase your circle of acquaintances, for both your sakes.'

Jack nodded. 'I shall do everything in

my power to find somewhere not too far away for us to live. You know how much I want Ellie to have her closest relatives around her.'

'You'll have plenty of support from all of us, Jack, that's for sure. But what I really meant to say was, take time to get to know Flora properly. Don't worry about bringing her to meet us until you're both completely easy in each other's company. And I wouldn't mention her to Ellie just yet.'

Jack hid a smile. Megan couldn't resist giving him just a tiny bit of advice. 'I was wondering about that,' he said. 'Ellie mightn't remember Flora anyway. Her mind was on other things.'

'Ducklings and baby lambs, probably.'

'As if she didn't have enough fluffy chicks around here.'

'She's a country girl, Jack. Unlike her mum, who couldn't wait to leave her green wellies behind and head off to the big city.'

They exchanged wry glances. 'But if

Charlotte hadn't done that, she and I would never have met. I'm a city boy at heart, aren't I?'

'I reckon so, but you've blended in beautifully here,' Megan replied.

'I do hope so. Just look at that sunset. It's practically an artist's palette. One of the things I enjoy about living here is the big sky.'

'Yes, we get excellent views of the heavens.'

Jack checked his watch. 'I think it's someone's bedtime.'

'And I'd better go to the kitchen and put the kettle on. Robbie and I can finish this wine tomorrow night while you're out on the town with Flora.'

* * *

Flora had already booked a hair appointment for the Saturday morning, more to have a trim than anything else. But now she had a date with the man of her dreams.

Her mother wasn't as ecstatic as Flora

was on hearing about the proposed outing. The two were in the kitchen, Flora washing up while her mum checked she had the right ingredients in her store cupboard for baking a Dundee cake.

'He's one of your regular passengers?' Mrs Petersen sounded doubtful. 'I suppose it's all right, but make sure you keep your phone with you at all times. You can always ring us from the ladies' room if you need rescuing. Dad will come and pick you up, you know that.'

'Mum,' Flora said patiently, 'Jack Slater's a friend of Trudy's husband. He's also been helpful to me on the train, and we've actually known each other quite a long time.'

'In a manner of speaking,' her mother said crisply. 'You know Tom's got engaged?'

'I hadn't heard, but I'm pleased for him,' said Flora. 'He didn't waste much time. Maybe she's a mail-order bride.'

'No, I think the young lady works at the garden centre,' her mother said.

'Not the post office.'

Flora didn't try to work out the logic, but couldn't help feeling relieved for Tom. She liked to think she'd kick-started his romance simply by putting an end to a very lukewarm relationship. Besides, she'd have made a hopeless farmer's wife, having been reprimanded by Tom for trying to give all the animals names and personalities.

She had no idea how things would work out between her and Jack, but an undeniable attraction existed. It was too soon to tell her mum about Ellie. That could wait. But Flora longed to see Jack's little daughter again, and loved the thought of spending time with her. She wouldn't dream of hinting how she felt, though. She'd waited quite a while for this day to arrive; and, amazingly, it seemed Mr Gorgeous had too. The sun was shining and her world had taken on a new aspect. It was time to wave goodbye to daydreams now she knew Jack Slater wanted to spend time getting to know her.

*　*　*

Next morning, Flora sang in the shower. She knew the words to more than one song from the musicals, but 'I'm in Love with a Wonderful Guy' summed up her feelings very well. She and her mother had watched old films many times over Flora's teenage years, and travelled to Cardiff a few years before to watch a touring production of *South Pacific*. She wondered, as she towelled herself dry, whether Jack shared her love of musical theatre. If not, what did it matter?

They had so much to find out about one another but the main thing was, their compatibility. She'd been clinging on to a relationship that was going nowhere, and now Jack's arrival in her life had sparked off a real attraction, she knew this wouldn't be like any random date. Jack came with emotional baggage. Would he compare her with Ellie's mum? For sure, she'd never be able to compete.

But Flora pushed dark thoughts away; and later, at the hairdresser's, she let her stylist trim her light brown hair and coax the ends under into a pageboy style. She'd always hankered after the look, but mostly wore her hair in a bouncy ponytail or sometimes a neat French pleat.

Maxine, the stylist who usually did her hair, seemed pleased with this change. 'You look so cool,' she said. 'My gran told me she wore this style in the late fifties, and I asked her to dig out some photographs. Would you mind if I took yours, for my portfolio?'

'I don't mind at all,' Flora said. 'So long as you don't post it on Facebook and places I probably don't even know about.'

'I wouldn't dream of such a thing,' said Maxine. 'Though if it happened to go viral, I'd love the publicity!' She grinned at Flora in the mirror.

'The very idea.' Flora made a face.

'Well, I'm sure your new look will go down well with your date this evening.

Is he a local boy?'

'He wasn't born round here, no.'

Maxine nodded. 'You're playing your cards close to your chest, and quite right too.' She held a hand mirror behind Flora's head so her client could see how she looked from the back.

'Oh thanks, Maxine, you've done a good job.' Flora twirled round in the revolving chair. 'I don't think Mum's forgiven me for abandoning Tom.'

'It was probably the best thing, under the circumstances.'

'I think so too. And if all goes well with my date, I'm sure your mum will find out when she next sees mine.'

'That'll probably be the Women's Institute meeting. My mum keeps on at me to join, but I really don't have time these days.'

'I think wives and mums nowadays have much more on their plates than their grandmas did.'

'Too true,' said Maxine. 'Even if my gran talks about hours spent polishing silver and brass, and making do with a titchy fridge and no freezer section when she was first married. Oh, and we try not to let her get started on disposable nappies!'

'You know, in some ways, I wish I'd been a teenager in the nineteen-fifties.' Flora spoke dreamily.

'Have you been watching too many old movies again?'

'Not for ages,' she admitted as Maxine helped her off with her salon gown. 'I'm mostly either at work or asleep these days.'

'But you enjoy your new job? I was so pleased to hear you'd got something so — well, so different. You must meet loads of people.'

'That's definitely true.'

'Can I ask whether your new boyfriend's a train driver or a passenger?'

'Wait until your mum's talked to my mum at the next WI meeting.'

'Flora Petersen, I know I shouldn't speak like this to one of my clients, but you really are a spoilsport!'

10

In her bedroom, luckily leaving herself plenty of time, Flora tried on three different outfits before making up her mind. Finally, she chose a vintage pale-blue-and-white polka-dot frock, worn over dark blue leggings and with a pair of navy blue shiny pumps. She didn't wear much make-up, but decided to use a misty blue eyeshadow and dark brown mascara to accentuate her eyes.

She checked the weather forecast and opted to wear a white jacket with elbow-length sleeves. She'd decided not to accept Jack's offer to collect her for the date, so the two were meeting inside the restaurant.

'How about I drop you down there, Flora?' her father offered. 'I thought I'd bring fish and chips back for a change, seeing as you're not eating with us.'

'That'd be great, thanks. But I hope you told Mum in good time, Dad!'

'I certainly did. You were still upstairs beautifying yourself, my girl. Mind you, it was well worth your efforts. What time are you meeting your young man?'

'He isn't my young man. This is our first date.' She glanced at her watch. 'And I must've misread my bedroom clock. I'm due there in ten minutes!'

'Let me pick up my wallet from the sideboard and we can go. You won't be late, love.'

But when she pushed open the door to Carl's Seafood Grill and Jack didn't come forward to greet her, she felt a tad nervous. Maybe something had happened to prevent him keeping their date. He'd never stand her up that was for sure. But as she gave his name to the waiter who greeted her, she did her best to look calm and confident and ignore the butterflies tap-dancing inside her.

As soon as she sat down at their reserved table and the waiter filled her water glass and brought two menus across, Flora took her phone from her handbag and checked her messages. Nothing. He must be on his way. Maybe Ellie hadn't wanted her daddy to go out? Maybe, as Flora had, he'd mistaken the time.

When the door opened, and Jack entered the restaurant looking for her, they met each other's gaze. He stopped looking anxious, and seemed so pleased to see her, she couldn't stop beaming. He even set off towards her before the waiter could greet him.

'Hello,' Jack said, stooping to kiss her cheek.

'Hello, yourself. I only just got here.'

'Thank goodness.' He sat down. 'I'll explain what kept me after we sort out some drinks. What would you like?'

She hadn't a clue. Her mind was blank. She was on a date with Mr Gorgeous, and he was driving, so she mustn't choose anything alcoholic. But Jack was already using his initiative.

'How about I order a bottle of wine? I got a lift here and I thought, if I call a taxi later, I can drop you off on the way.' He looked expectantly at her.

'Well, if you're sure. I got a lift too.'

'Perfect. A bottle of white, then?'

'Fine by me.'

Jack glanced down the wine list. 'There's a nice Australian Sauvignon here — or how about a Welsh vintage?' He looked up and smiled.

'I'd prefer you chose, Jack. It'll be safer that way.'

'All right, let's go for the Welsh Chardonnay. Apparently it has a palate of grapefruit, wet stone and vanilla cream!'

'Wow, I wonder who thinks up these descriptions?'

'We'll live dangerously for once.' Jack handed the green leather folder back to the waiter who bustled off.

'Did you have a good day with Ellie?' Flora asked.

'Um, sort of,' he said. 'Um, I was just — you've done something to your hair, haven't you? You look lovely. Not that you don't usually look nice, I mean.'

Flora tried to help him. 'Top marks for noticing,' She put her head on one side and looked at him. 'You scrub up well yourself — and I do believe your hair's looking different too.'

'Well spotted! I went to the barber's. It's the first time in ages I've felt I should do something about my image.' He pulled a face. 'I haven't exactly been keeping pace with fashion.'

She was admiring the way his shirt matched his blue eyes, but didn't want to sound too gushing. Now there was an awkward silence, and she knew if she referred to the reason behind his remark, it would dampen down an evening still hardly begun.

'Even though I worked in a dress shop for years, I've always had a liking for retro stuff.'

'Is that like vintage? Is that what you're wearing?'

'Kind of . . . I enjoy mixing eras.'

Their wine arrived. Flora sat back

while the waiter and Jack interacted; until, left alone once more, she raised her glass to chink against his.

'Here's to the future,' he said.

'That's an uncertain kind of thing to toast.'

'Maybe. But at last I'm looking forward to it,' he said. 'Maybe things will start going my way now.'

She felt something stir within her, and she didn't think it was only the effect of the cool, slightly honeyed wine she was sipping and enjoying.

'I'm glad you feel like that,' she said. 'It's good we both have things to look forward to.'

He put down his wineglass. 'We need to decide what we want to eat. Then maybe we can learn a little more about one another. There's so much I want to ask you.'

Flora smiled. 'Me too.' But now the big moment had arrived, she couldn't help fearing he might be disappointed once he discovered how boring she really was.

Next time Flora met Trudy for lunch, they both arrived at the train conductors' mess room on time.

'I'm longing to hear how your date went.' Trudy put her tray on the table and pulled out a chair.

'You're probably going to kill me,' Flora said gloomily, taking the seat opposite.

'Not before I find out how you got on with Mr Gorgeous. And why would I want to kill you?'

Flora reached for the black pepper. 'You'll soon find out.'

'Well, you've chosen a ham salad today, so you can't be comfort eating. That has to be a good sign.' Trudy, who'd opted for battered cod and chips, was bashing the bottom of the ketchup bottle. 'Come on, Flora. What's his name?'

'Jack.'

Trudy looked up. 'Jack what?'

'Jack Slater.'

'You're joking! Not the same Jack Slater that my husband knows?'

'Yes.' Flora broke into her crispy white bread roll.

Trudy gave a low whistle. 'Well, there's a coincidence. But that's great,' she said. 'Isn't it?'

'It took me a while to realise, because I didn't know his name until the train broke down in the middle of nowhere. I was on my way to meet my aunt and he came to find me.'

Trudy raised her eyebrows. 'Did he, now!'

'He said he caught a glimpse of me waiting on the platform. He gets on at the stop before; and I wasn't in uniform, of course.'

'Mmm.'

'What does that mean?'

'I think it proves Jack's rather shy. He'd probably been sitting there, wondering whether to go and speak to you or not. Then, when the delay was announced, he must have thought: why not go for it, and see if the beautiful maiden is waiting for her Prince Charming to appear!'

Flora spluttered on her soft drink. 'You nearly made me choke — but not like I did on Saturday evening, thank goodness.'

'Hang on,' Trudy said, 'what made you choke? Also, for the second time, I'd like to know why you've decided I might need to kill you.' She speared a couple of chips and popped them in her mouth.

'I chose a chicken dish that was totally lush, served with jasmine rice and lovely fresh veggies. Jack was eating steak with all the trimmings, and he was asking me where I liked to go on holiday, and suddenly my throat tightened up and a chunk of chicken lodged where it shouldn't.'

'It went down the wrong way? Poor you.'

'I couldn't speak or breathe, and I started coughing but it came out with the most horrible sound; so I jumped up, pushed my chair back, and ran to the ladies' room.'

'Someone must have thumped you on the back?'

Flora shuddered. 'I realise now, of course, I shouldn't have left the table. When I charged into the ladies' room there was nobody there, and that's when I felt really scared.'

'You should've dashed straight out again, Flora!'

'Luckily, I didn't need to, because Jack followed me. He burst through the door, got behind me and gave me a good thump.'

'Wow, he was definitely your knight in shining armour. Thank goodness he didn't just stay at the table.'

'It doesn't bear thinking about.'

'But I still don't get why you aren't over the moon about him. Is it that he's nice but boring?'

Flora heaved a sigh and put down her cutlery. 'He's definitely not boring, and I'm still crazy about him. He's absolutely gorgeous, and I've never ever felt like this before about anyone.'

'So what's your problem?'

Flora suppressed a sob. 'I think I'm too ordinary for him. That's why I was so anxious to impress, I suppose.'

It was a relief to share her feelings with her friend. Trudy wouldn't tell her not to be stupid. Trudy, with her interesting past career in aviation and her greater experience of life and men, made the perfect guru for Flora — and was also fun to be with. But today Flora appeared to have silenced her. Neither spoke for a while.

Trudy finished her meal, then looked across at Flora. 'Tell me exactly what you mean by 'too ordinary'?'

'There's nothing special about me. I know you'll probably think I'm stupid, but while we were at the restaurant, I coaxed Jack to tell me about Ellie's mum.'

'It sounds as though he didn't want to talk about her. Was this before you had the choking fit or afterwards?'

'Afterwards. It was such a lovely meal, but I didn't feel like flirting or trying to think of interesting things to say, so I was trying to get him to tell me a bit about Charlotte.'

'It must have been awful for you, but I expect it wasn't too good for Jack either, once he realised you might choke to death.' Trudy shuddered.

'I know. He was very kind, and I think he actually enjoyed our date more than I did.'

'But why do you say that?' Trudy checked her watch. 'I need to go soon, but I don't like to think of you feeling so miserable. I know how much you like Mr Gorgeous — I mean, Jack. Did he ask if he could see you again?'

'I can't think why, but yes, he did.'

'There you are then. Your fears are unfounded. But I'd still like to know why you have such a low opinion of yourself.'

'Because, having heard all about Charlotte, I can't understand what he can possibly see in me.'

'Ah. I don't wish to sound too critical, but you and Jack are right at the start of what will hopefully become a loving relationship. It's important for you both to get to know one another and concentrate on the moment rather than looking back — in his case, to his marriage; and in yours, to your long relationship with the farmer guy.'

'Tom probably asked me out in the first place because he's quite boring himself!'

'Not up to me to comment. Circumstances didn't cause you to stop seeing him, so things drifted along until you lost your job — and look what's happened since then.'

'It's been amazing.' Flora managed a smile.

'Precisely. And if you were boring, you wouldn't be such a hit with the passengers, now, would you?' She paused. 'No, don't answer that — you'd only disagree, and that would be really silly. Remember, I haven't known you very long, but I've helped train you and I've heard people speak well of you; quite frankly, it's no surprise to me that

Jack asked you out. And don't put yourself down. Jack sounds as if he has excellent taste in women, and that's a great compliment to you.'

'D'you really think so?'

'I do indeed. Now, I have to go, but I want you to put all those negative thoughts out of your head. So the first date wasn't all hearts and flowers? I wouldn't mind betting the second one will turn out to be much, much easier.' She gathered her bag and jacket together. 'Alright now, petal?'

Flora laughed. 'That must be, considering what my name is, the worst pun I've ever heard, Trudy!'

11

Flora set off from Parkswell, feeling happier after her heart-to-heart with Trudy. But she hadn't wanted to reveal she was still haunted by the possibility of Jack regretting becoming involved with someone he'd find it difficult to avoid meeting on his journeys to and from his office. He'd held her hand in the taxi home while they chatted about stuff her dad would probably describe as small talk, before the driver stopped at her house, and Jack hopped out to give her a hug and a peck on the cheek before she went inside. He'd promised to be in touch, but so far she hadn't heard anything; although it was still only Monday, and she knew she mustn't expect miracles. Yet how she longed to see him again and watch his blue eyes sparkle when he looked at her. If he was on the train today, this particular service was the one he normally used; and as he'd be using the return half of his day ticket, they couldn't possibly avoid contact with one another.

The passenger load varied, with some sections of the journey being busier than others, and Flora had her work cut out for her, keeping track of people boarding and making sure she checked all the new passengers' tickets. Some people were changing trains and wanted confirmation about the rest of their journeys. Some were in the mood for a chat, but this wasn't the right afternoon for that. Finally, on one of the longer sections, she found time for a cup of tea as well as an opportunity to check her phone.

Jack had texted her! Flora held her breath as his message appeared on her screen. Before they parted, he'd asked when she was next working the train, and she'd told him which days she was rostered. But he might have decided to use his car for a while, to let things settle, and to avoid embarrassing either of them. She felt sure he was that kind of person, and wouldn't want to vanish from her life without some kind of explanation.

But what Jack wrote bore no resemblance to the scenario she'd fabricated in her mind.

Hi Flora, hope you're well. Sorry I shan't see you today. ☹ Ellie has chickenpox so we spent a difficult Sunday. Working from home today, to give Gran a break. See you tomorrow, I hope. ☺ P.S. I've had chickenpox. xx Those two kisses caused Flora to read it through another time.

Her reply was brief. I have too! Sorry to hear about Ellie. Speak soon. xx

Flora pressed 'Send', feeling a whole lot happier than she had before receiving Jack's text.

* * *

'I was convinced I'd frighten you away!' Jack had boarded the train and waited for Flora to check all was in order before she got on and secured the last door.

'Frighten me away?' She longed for a hug but knew that was out of the question.

'Yes, by mentioning the chickenpox.'

'But we've both already had it, haven't we?'

'Sure. What I meant was, when you start going out with someone and he hasn't only got himself to think of, socialising sometimes has to take a back seat. Kids get these ailments, and parents have to jump to it.'

'Your working arrangements are flexible, Jack. It's fortunate you can change your schedule and help care for your little girl.'

'Ellie was quite out of sorts on Sunday, poor love.'

'It can be a miserable disease, but better for little ones to get it over with. Is she better today?'

'Her gran says so.' He glanced around. 'I'd better find a seat. It's so good to see you again, Flora.'

She swallowed hard. 'You too. It's funny, but I was also wondering if you were having second thoughts.'

'Don't even think about it.' He spoke so quietly, she was glad she'd managed to lip-read. The train was picking up speed again, rattling over the points, and the refreshment trolley was lumbering through the next carriage.

'Is it alright if I ring you tonight?'

'That would be lovely.' Flora smiled at him. 'After eight o'clock is best, if that's OK.'

'I'll have done the bedtime story bit by then.'

'That's the most important thing for you to do, Jack. Don't hurry it because of me, please.'

He smiled down at her. 'Bless you, Flora. You don't know how good it is to hear you say that.' He glanced round. 'I'm going to stand here and buy a coffee before your colleague goes through to the next coach.'

'And I must get on with my work! Speak later then.'

Flora set off to check on passengers who'd boarded at the last station. Outside, the weather was turning gloomy, evening mist creeping and curling around the cattle she saw grazing in a distant field. But in Flora's world, things were looking brighter again. Trudy had been right, thank goodness. Flora knew what was happening to her, and if she truly was falling deeper and deeper in love, she wanted with all her heart for Jack to tumble headlong with her.

The remainder of the journey passed without any awkward incidents or alarms. Flora said goodbye to Jack, and waved him on his way on arrival at Redbush. She looked forward to catching up when he rang her later; but, with his small daughter in the throes of chickenpox, it was unlikely he'd suggest they went out again over the next week or so. When the service arrived at Broadland, Flora's home base, she left the train and headed for the office.

'Hey, Flora!'

Startled, she turned round to see Gareth walking towards her.

'Fancy seeing you here,' she said. 'Are you taking this one back?'

'For my sins!' He grinned. 'I don't need to check in yet. I don't suppose you fancy a little stroll?'

★ ★ ★

Jack drove back from the station on an evening which belonged in one of those atmospheric movies where mist blurs the edges and plays tricks with the eyesight. He needed his headlights on half-beam, and he kept alert to the possibility of walkers on the minor roads or a stray animal appearing in the middle of the highway. On such an evening, creepy background music would be highly appropriate.

But his mood wasn't at all dismal. Not now he'd caught up with Flora and had the phone call to look forward to later. Not that it was much use asking if she'd like to go out with him again.

That would be pushing things too far regarding childcare, though he knew his in-laws would move mountains for him and their grand-daughter. Luckily, Flora seemed to understand how things were, but he wondered why such an attractive and pleasant young woman didn't possess a string of young men queuing up to take her out. Maybe he'd find out. Sadly, her choking fit at the restaurant had spoilt the evening for her, though he'd assured her all that mattered was her being safe. But he didn't like the way she'd doubted he would want to see her again. He smiled at the way they'd each felt similarly. What were they like, the pair of them! Hopefully, they could go forward now, and boost one another's confidence.

He slowed for a bend sharp as a fiddler's elbow, and drove cautiously round it. It would suit him far better to live somewhere nearer civilisation, as long as he was still within the area. Ellie attended a medium-sized primary school and was happy there. No way did he want to upset that particular applecart; but when house-hunting, he needed to balance convenience with quality of life. He wouldn't take his daughter with him when he began viewings, as she might find that unsettling. As soon as he found what he considered to be the perfect house — he couldn't seem to think of it as a home — he intended taking her to see it and watch her reaction. Maybe take her gran along as well, if she could spare the time. And if they all felt the same, he'd make an offer.

So, when should he tell his daughter about Flora? One part of him couldn't wait. The other more cautious part would rather come face to face with one of the scary monsters in that pop-up picture book that used to belong to Ellie's mum, and which his daughter adored with all the passion of a six-year-old.

He pulled up on the forecourt of his in-laws' house. It was an idyllic spot, a smallholding they'd bought many years before. Ellie's gran kept hens, and ran a small business providing eggs to local customers. Robbie grew vegetables and fruit that he also sold locally. Yet they'd taken in Jack and Ellie with not a moment's hesitation. They were what he thought of as the salt of the earth, and he knew they were going to miss their grand-daughter once she and her dad moved out. But he mustn't outstay his welcome. The future looked a whole lot brighter now Flora was on the scene, though he knew he mustn't rush her. His newfound joy was tinged with more than a mild feeling of panic. Relationships were far more difficult for him to navigate than any rules or regulations concerning planning and mapping.

He picked up his canvas satchel and got out of his car. Before he headed in through the back door, he walked a few yards across the gravelled surface of the yard. The phone signal around the smallholding was nothing to write home about, and Jack always hoped to find a magic spot where he'd feel connected to the world, but so far without success. This evening was no different.

At least he'd be able to use the landline to call Flora later. He could take one of the phones up to his room so he had privacy — and maybe, just maybe, dare to suggest that he and she might pencil in a date when they could meet again, perhaps visiting one of the ancient castles or botanical gardens in the area. Walking round soaking up the scenery might make for a more relaxed outing than a restaurant.

'It's me,' Jack called, closing the door behind him.

His daughter came running from the sitting room. 'Daddy, you're back! I've missed you.'

Swallowing a lump in his throat, Jack swung Ellie up in his arms. 'Hello, Miss Spotty Face! You seem a lot better.'

She giggled. 'Hello, Mr Daddy Face! Gran made me a strawberry jelly today. You can have some, if you're good.'

'Wow, thank you very much. Is it a rabbit-shaped jelly?'

She nodded. He lowered her gently to the floor. 'Phew, you're getting heavier, Ellie. Too much jelly!'

His mother-in-law appeared in the doorway. 'Jack, there's tea in the pot, and some flapjacks if you can't last out till supper.'

'Hi, Megan. Thank you so much. How's your day been?' Briefly, Jack thought about how his domestic life might be when he and Ellie lived in their new house. He pushed the thought away.

'Pretty good, thanks. Oh, while I think of it, our phone's out of order.'

At once he felt cold inside, and bitterly disappointed. 'You mean the landline?'

'Afraid so. Were you planning on using it this evening?'

'I, um, yes. I was hoping to ring a friend around eight o'clock.' He knew Megan realised which friend he meant as soon as she shot him a sympathetic look. 'Have you reported the fault?'

'Robbie went over to the neighbours' and used their phone. It's a pain, but we've been told things should be back to normal tomorrow.' She hesitated. 'All I can suggest is that you go out after supper and park in that layby along the main road. You can pick up a reasonable signal there.'

12

Flora checked her watch. 'I've left my father's car in the car park, so I mustn't be too long. Was there any special reason for wanting to talk to me, Gareth?'

'Should there be? Am I treading on anyone's toes?'

Flora decided not to pick up on this comment. She hoped he wasn't referring to what she thought he was. She and Jack were at far too early a stage of their relationship for her to mention she already had a boyfriend. Maybe Gareth wanted to discuss something entirely different.

'All right. I just need to sign off duty, then maybe you can walk to the car park with me so I can lock my bag in the boot? I'm afraid I don't have time to go for a coffee.'

'No worries.' He fell into step with

her. 'Still enjoying the job?'

'Very much. I realise it wouldn't be everyone's cup of tea, but I like the feeling of being on the move. You wouldn't think so, after years spent working in a shop.'

'The only trouble is, social life can get a little tricky when we're all working different shifts.'

'Tricky? In what way?'

Gareth groaned. 'Come on, Flora, let's not play games with each other. I've been thinking about you for a while now. You don't seem too upset if we happen to bump into one another. So, how about coming out with me sometime?'

They'd reached her dad's car. Flora had been about to use her key. Now she stopped.

'I'm being thoughtless, you've been on your feet all day,' Gareth said. 'If you unlock the car, we can sit inside for a few minutes.' He took a step closer and held out his hand. 'Here, let me do it for you.'

Flora looked around her. Why did she feel uneasy? She was used to Gareth teasing her, but he'd always seemed laid-back, always treating her like she'd expect him to treat a colleague. This evening he seemed different. Or could it be that she was misreading the signals? She felt at a disadvantage. She needed to think on her feet.

'It's OK, thanks.' She checked her watch again. 'Goodness, I didn't realise that was the time! I need to get Dad's car back, or he'll be late going out. It's quiz night at the local pub and he's in a team. I'm sure to see you on the changeover some time soon.'

Gareth grabbed her arm. 'But you've been sending me signals. What's up with you?'

Flora took a deep breath. This was serious stuff. There was nobody else around. She hated the thought of any unpleasantness, but she was determined to stand up for herself, even if this man had his eye on her.

'Please let go of me.' She gazed

steadily at him and he released her arm immediately.

'I apologise if I've given you any cause to encourage you, Gareth, though I can't think of any occasion where I have. Can we just forget this ever happened and continue as we were, please?'

'Flipping heck! You're a funny girl, Flora. You sound like somebody out of one of those cloak-and-bonnet dramas my mum watches on TV.'

She smiled. 'Thanks for the compliment. In many ways, I think I'd be more suited to another era.'

'I don't know about that. I'd better let you get your dad's car back; but what a waste of a lovely girl. We could have a really good time together, I just know it.'

Flora looked away, uncertain how to react.

He sucked in his breath. 'There's someone else, isn't there? You already have a fella, and yet you thought it'd be fun to lead me on!'

She felt a flash of anger. 'I did not! I thought you were a mate. I thought you wanted a bit of company and some fresh air before going on duty again. And my personal life's none of your business!'

She pointed her key at the car and heard the click. She opened the driver's door and got in. Gareth knocked on the window. She pressed the down button and waited for him to speak.

'Better not drive off without your bag, Miss Pride and Prejudice. I'll put it on the back seat. No hard feelings?'

'Thank you. No hard feelings.' She waited for him to close the door.

Flora drove home, feeling foolish. They talked about the games people played, but somehow she didn't know the rules. Should she have told Gareth straight away about Jack Slater? Told him she'd better not even take a walk alone with another man? Now, that really *was* straight from a Jane Austen novel. She'd need to swear Trudy to secrecy, but she could do with a bit of advice. Working locally and dating a farmer had cushioned her from the big wide world, but now she was out there, and at the moment felt very unsettled.

When Jack rang her later, she decided she wouldn't mention what had happened. He might think she was trying to rush him into saying something he wasn't intending to say. But she couldn't wait to get his call and end her day on a cheerful note.

★ ★ ★

Did children possess superhero powers? As if knowing her daddy had something else on his mind, Ellie picked at her supper, and Jack needed all his powers of patience and diplomacy to coax her into a warm bath before her bedtime.

The little girl fussed over having enough bubbles and insisted her gran came to pat her dry, making her daddy feel a little sidelined, hoping his fatherly skills weren't falling short of the mark. But once Ellie was in her

150

pyjamas and clutching Freddie the teddy, she quickly scrambled up on Jack's lap to listen to more adventures of the lucky children who'd discovered the amazing enchanted wood and its fabulous occupants.

His small daughter was very drowsy when Jack put her gently to bed. He stayed beside her until her eyelids no longer fluttered open to check if he was still there. Only when he went downstairs again did he glance through the window and receive a shock.

Robbie looked up from the auction catalogue he was reading. 'Job to see your hand in front of your face out there.'

Jack raised his eyebrows. 'When did this come on? It was nowhere near as bad when I drove back from the station.'

'It's been getting steadily worse. You weren't thinking of going out, were you, son?'

Jack grimaced. 'I need to make a phone call. Megan suggested I went along to that layby to pick up a signal.'

'Can't it wait until tomorrow? Or how about emailing whoever it is you need to speak to?'

Jack shook his head. 'I promised to call this evening, and I don't know her email address. I hate the thought of letting her down.' He hadn't meant to let that information slip, and stood, waiting for his father-in-law to comment.

'I see.' Robbie gazed at Jack. 'I understand how you must feel, but you'd be putting your life at risk, taking your car out in a pea-souper like that. They gave a warning on the local news not long ago.'

'I hadn't a clue the fog had clamped down like that.' Jack shook his head again.

'You'd other things on your mind. It's bad luck the phone's out of order, but these things happen, Jack. Whoever it is will understand, surely?'

'It's not as simple as that.'

'Why don't you sit down and tell me

about it. Or are you afraid I won't understand?' His eyes were kindly.

Jack sat down opposite him. 'Has Megan said anything?'

Robbie chuckled. 'Of course not! You know she wouldn't want you to think we were talking about you behind your back.'

'It's not easy — trying to move on, yet not wanting to make a mistake.'

'You and Charlotte made a good team. But she wouldn't expect you to shut yourself off from another relationship. As for making mistakes, I'm afraid none of us can guard against doing that.'

'That's what Megan said, more or less. I'm lucky you two understand. The most important person is Ellie, of course.'

'At the moment, I'd suggest the most important person is the young lady you're hoping to talk to.'

Jack smiled at last. 'Yeah, good point. I'm getting round to realising how important Flora is to me. I hope — I think — she feels the same way.'

'How long have you known her?'

'Funnily enough, we've been glimpsing one another for several months now, but we only got friendlier recently. She's a train conductor, and she works on the route I use.'

'Is that right? So, she must have experienced delays and mishaps if she does a lot of travelling?'

'Yes, but I can't just sit here and let her think I've forgotten my promise to ring.' He glanced at the window. 'I think I'll walk to the layby. What d'you reckon?'

'I'm relieved you're not thinking of driving; but on that stretch before you get to the main road, you'll need to take very great care. There are always idiots around, remember.'

'I'll take a flashlight, and I can put on that yellow oilskin hanging in the utility room. Is that OK?'

'Hmm ... not a lot of point my arguing with you. Remember, weather conditions can affect phone signals, but

I don't want to pour cold water over your plan. To be honest . . . back in the day, in these circumstances, if I'd needed to find a phone box so I could ring Megan, I'd have done the same thing as you.'

'Thank you.' Jack jumped up. 'It should only take me about twenty minutes.'

'You'll need to mind where you tread, and make sure you keep tight to the hedgerow. At least the milk lorry won't be coming through at this time of the evening.'

'I'll be very, very careful. Thanks again, Robbie.' Jack headed towards the door.

'You better had, son,' his father-in-law called after him. 'You really better had!'

*   *   *

Jack, feeling a little like a teenager disobeying his parents, let himself out of the back door at a quarter to eight. Hopefully, he might pick up a signal a bit before the layby. The fog, he decided, was daunting enough to put off most sane people; but he was blessed with good eyesight, and he'd shoved a small torch in one pocket and carried a powerful flashlight in his hand. He turned left out of the gate and walked steadily. Luckily, he'd thought to put on a pair of sturdy gloves, ready to push back any trailing brambles waiting to rip into his clothing.

There wasn't a sound anywhere. Just the steady tread of his boots on the road. When he walked on an uneven patch of highway, gravel spurted and rattled beneath his feet, but he concentrated on watching the beam of light ahead of him. The hoot of an owl startled him, but he still kept on walking. If only he possessed the same powers as the big bird — then he'd have no fear of becoming disorientated.

An eerie, thick nothingness all around him shrouded the entire countryside, and he daren't risk wandering further out in the road. Fortunately,

Jack met no vehicles either approaching from behind or oncoming; and, with an enormous sense of relief, reached the signboard at the junction between the road from his in-laws' smallholding and the main highway. Here, he paused beneath the sign and took out his phone to check it.

'Not a sausage,' he said, putting it away again. 'Talking to myself now. Don't they say that's one of the first signs? Oh, Flora, please don't think I'm playing games with you.'

But should he really risk continuing? Robbie's last comment still echoed in his head. No matter how careful he tried to be, he was still at the mercy of the elements.

Jack stood at the junction, aiming his torch beam downwards while he considered his options. Should he be a wimp and turn back? Or should he continue along the main road? If so, he needed to take a left and cross to the other side so he faced any oncoming traffic.

He was scolding himself for being indecisive when he realised the beam of the flashlight didn't seem as powerful as it had when he started out. While he was concentrating on testing it, moving the beam this way and that, he suddenly realised he could hear the roar of an engine. And it sounded perilously close.

13

After supper, Flora changed from her uniform into a pair of pink-and-white polka-dot pyjamas and pushed her feet into towelling mules. Her father had gone out to join his teammates for the monthly pub quiz and her mother was watching *Casablanca* — probably, as she'd joked with Flora, for the millionth time. Flora, a great fan of the iconic film, would normally have joined her; but after watching the opening scenes, she drifted away into the kitchen to brew some tea while she kept watch on her phone. It sat in the middle of the kitchen table, but as the hands of the clock moved ever closer to eight, she felt a glow of expectancy, knowing she'd soon hear Jack's voice.

She gave the tea a stir, put the lid back on the pot and sat down, pulling her mum's favourite magazine towards her. Flora caught her breath as she drank in the scene featured on its cover.

The Western Highland landscape, captured at sunset, beneath a plum, raspberry and peacock-blue sky, looked ravishing. She was used to beautiful scenery, having lived in west Wales all her life — but how lovely it would be to one day visit the place her grandmother had been born. She couldn't stop a little smile teasing her lips at the thought of making the trip with Jack and his small daughter.

Stop trying to live in the future! She muttered the advice to herself as she poured tea into two mugs. But when she returned after taking her mum's drink to her, the phone still remained silent. Flora reminded herself that she'd suggested it was better not to call her before eight o'clock, so Jack was only doing what she'd asked. She would, of course, have dropped everything to speak to him; but with her dad going out, she knew her mother would wait to eat with her, and it would have seemed churlish if she'd left the table to speak in private.

She flicked through the pages of the magazine, sipping her tea and nibbling a dark chocolate digestive biscuit — naughty, but nice. Yet by half past eight, Flora was certain she must have the wrong end of the stick. Maybe she was the one supposed to do the ringing? But, recalling their conversation on board the train, she knew she wasn't mistaken. Jack would surely never play around with her emotions. A frisson of fear rippled down her spine as she wondered if something was wrong with Ellie. Children sometimes fell ill and recovered again with astonishing speed, judging by what she'd heard from friends and relations.

She was reaching for her phone, intending to send him a text, when, hearing her mother call from the sitting room, she got up and went to see what she wanted.

'This is absolutely my favourite bit.'

Her mum's gaze was riveted on the screen.

Flora perched on the edge of the settee. 'I can never understand why, when it's so dreadfully sad.'

She noticed her mum reaching for a tissue. Together, they watched the co-stars gazing into each other's eyes. The aeroplane, poised to take off from Morocco on a gloomy wartime night, loomed in the background.

'Two people who loved one another, facing the anguish of a final parting,' Flora murmured.

'And at a time in history when no one knew what further horrors war might bring,' her mother said.

Flora felt the poignancy and the hopelessness of the situation even more than she had on other occasions when watching the film. She gulped and bit back a sob. Why was she torturing herself like this? It was only a film, for goodness' sake!

She tiptoed from the room, unnoticed by her mum. Back in the kitchen, she took out her phone and typed a message to Jack.

Hope everything's OK. Speak soon? xx

She sent the message and drank the remainder of her tea, wrinkling her nose on discovering how much it had cooled. But on looking at her phone again, she found unwelcome news. Her text hadn't been delivered. Something was wrong, and she couldn't do a thing about it until Jack made contact.

* * *

As soon as the juggernaut's headlights became visible, Jack's survival instinct kicked in. He had no time to do anything else but squeeze his body against the hedgerow. The narrow grassy strip beside the highway didn't feel the best place to be with a lumbering great truck bearing down on him.

Now, wedged into a hedgerow containing too many sharp-toothed brambles, he winced as a thorn tore his chin. Jack closed his eyes, raising his gloved hands to protect his face while he slowly extricated himself. He could see the glow of the big vehicle's emergency lights flashing ahead. The driver had stopped, and moments later, Jack heard a door bang.

'You alright, mate?' a concerned voice called.

'Yeah, I think I might look as though I've been in a fight, though!'

The bulky dark figure of a man emerged through the fog. 'You gave me a bit of a scare, old son. Where are you trying to get to?'

Jack removed the last spiteful bramble from his sleeve. 'This might sound daft, but I'm hoping to find a signal so I can make a phone call.'

'Is this an emergency? If so, I can use the company's radio band.'

'Um, no, it's not, but thanks for offering.' He tried to think of something that wouldn't sound too ridiculous.

'Girlfriend?'

'Let's just say she's a special friend.'

'So, do you want a lift to wherever it is? You'll be safer riding with me than walking along the road on a night like this.'

Jack's mind was made up. 'That'd be great. About a mile further on, there's a layby. If you could drop me there, please?'

'No problem. It's my first time working this route — just my luck for the weather to play up. Worse for you, though, being out in it.'

The driver led the way to the passenger side, and opened the door so Jack could clamber up, before joining him in the cab. After they pulled away, Jack strained his eyes trying to peer through the gloom. Landmarks, not that there were many, appeared to be obliterated by the murkiness.

'There it is,' the driver said, slowing down. 'Unless you want to play safe and go on to the next town?'

'No thanks,' Jack said, suppressing his concern over the flashlight's lifespan. 'If I can hop out here, I'll try my phone and hope for the best.'

'Rather you than me, mate. Mind how you go, now.' He pulled into the layby and came to a halt.

Jack watched the lorry's rear lights disappear without trace. Even the engine sound was swallowed up within moments, and he hadn't noticed any other vehicle pass by for quite a while. He took his phone from his pocket, noting the time. Flora would be wondering what had happened to him. And if he didn't make his way back soon, Robbie would start considering whether to come in search of him. No way did he want to cause that.

The signal wasn't wonderful here, but it was better than nothing, and well worth a try.

* * *

Flora was back in the sitting room, watching the final action of the film as the aircraft bearing Rick's true love taxied away, leaving him on a very foggy night in Casablanca.

'You seem a bit fidgety, dear.' Flora's mum said, picking up the TV remote control. 'I thought I'd watch that quiz show I like now.'

'I'll leave you to it, Mum. I'm expecting a phone call. Jack said he'd ring, but it's way past the time I was expecting to hear.'

Her mother glanced at the window. 'It's a bit foggy out there. I hope your dad doesn't have trouble getting home.'

Flora stared at her. 'I wonder if it's the same where Jack lives. He must've got back from the station all right, surely.'

'No good worrying,' her mum said. 'Have you tried ringing?'

'I sent him a text, but all I got was an 'undeliverable' message.'

'Can't be doing with those things.'

'I know you can't, Mum. But messaging's very useful, and works most of the time.'

'Doesn't this Jack have a proper phone?'

'Yes, I expect there's a landline. All I have is his mobile number, though.'

'Why not look him up on one of those online directories?'

Flora blinked in surprise. 'Mum, you're a genius.' Her expression changed. 'Except I've just realised I haven't a clue what name to look for. Jack lives with his late wife's parents, you see.'

Her mother bit her lip. 'I see. Oh well, then I suppose all you can do is wait, love.'

★ ★ ★

Jack called up Flora's phone number, breathing a sigh of relief as he heard it ringing.

She picked up almost at once. 'Jack? Is everything alright?'

'I'm fine, but I know I'm late calling you. Sorry, Flora. The landline's down, back at the house.' Swiftly, he explained the setbacks he'd had.

'Poor you,' Flora said. 'I'm sorry you've had so much hassle, but I was worried something might be wrong with Ellie.'

He chuckled softly. 'She's right as rain, thanks. It's nice of you to think of her.'

'I can't help it. She's part of you.'

Jack swallowed hard, unable to believe this lovely girl could possibly feel for him as he did for her. Flora's words had come tumbling out, reminding him of her warmth and thoughtfulness. He counted himself lucky. But he was hopeless at letting his feelings show, especially when standing outside on a murky night in what, on a bad day, he sometimes referred to as the back of beyond.

'Flora, I want to tell you that I've, um, I've spoken about you to Ellie's grandparents. About you and me, I mean.'

'I see. I do realise that can't have been easy for you, Jack. Or for them, either.'

'I told Megan first. She was absolutely great. Robbie found out this evening because I needed to explain why I wanted to go out on such a miserable night. He's not dim — soon realised how important you are to me.'

'Thank you for telling me. I think Mum twigged something when I couldn't settle tonight, even though she was watching one of my favourite films.'

'So nothing contemporary, then,' he teased.

'*Casablanca.*'

He laughed. 'As recent as that! Great film.' For moments, he imagined himself and Flora snuggled up on a sofa, watching it together.

'Lots of fog at the end, so very appropriate! It sounds as though the weather's really bad where you are.'

'Flora,' Jack said, 'I'd have walked through a blizzard to talk to you! When can we meet? And I don't mean on the train. My sister-in-law would happily have Ellie to stay over for a weekend. We could spend a whole day together. If you'd like to, I mean,' he ended in a hurry, hoping he wasn't rushing her.

'That sounds perfect. But I wouldn't

want your little girl to feel left out.'

'She always adores going to her auntie's, so don't worry. I'm hoping Ellie and I can get together with you some time soon, but for the moment I'd rather like to keep you to myself.'

'I'd like that, but what about your house-hunting? You must find it difficult to view places unless it's a Saturday.'

He hesitated, having forgotten how convoluted it could be when beginning a new relationship. He didn't want to sound too presumptuous, but he wanted Flora to know how special she was. How he didn't regard her as only a casual girlfriend. He decided not to beat around the bush, and hope he didn't frighten her away.

'I'll manage. I can be flexible over my hours now and then. Some vendors leave a key with their agent if they're out all day. And when I find a couple of houses that appeal, if it's at all possible I'd like to take you with me for my second viewing.'

Flora sucked in her breath. That was unexpected, but maybe he preferred a second opinion from someone outside his family. 'I'd love to come along with you. I think I'm off-duty the next weekend but one. Shall I text you to confirm? Just in case we don't meet on the train.'

'Please, Flora.'

'You must get back now. Take care, Jack.'

'You bet. I think the fog isn't quite so dense, but I'll go carefully, never fear. Night-night — ' He hesitated before adding, ' — my darling.'

Jack closed the call and switched on the flashlight, zapping the small torch into life too before setting off back down the road home. It seemed to him both lights shone brightly, rather like his hope for a future. A future that included something he hadn't dared imagine might happen. And that something was a very special young woman indeed.

14

Flora became an owner-driver after her dad helped her pick out a modest second-hand car. They'd researched online and found something locally that seemed suitable. She was driving herself to and from the station now, and relishing her independence.

Luckily, her parents were tolerant over what she gave them towards her keep, but she didn't want them to go to the other extreme.

'We enjoy having you at home, Flora,' her mum said after Flora transferred some money to her parents' joint account. 'Dad told me what you paid in and we both think it's far too much.'

'I don't think it is, Mum,' Flora insisted. 'I'm working again, and Dad's helped me with the car too, don't forget.'

'We'll talk about it some other time. Shouldn't you be off now, dear? I imagine you don't want to be late for your date. And you look very pretty, Flora. Jack's a lucky young man.'

Flora hugged her mother. 'It works both ways, Mum.'

'I do worry that he has a young daughter. It does seem a pity things didn't work out for you and Tom.'

She didn't have time for this. 'Mum, you're absolutely right. I need to go, or I'll miss my train and keep Jack waiting.' She was driving to Broadland, then Jack would meet her train at Jamesbridge so they could go on to Roseland Manor, a wonderful old house set in a particularly interesting garden.

'Have a lovely time, dear.'

Flora hurried from the house, still fretting over her mother's attitude. Why wouldn't she accept that Tom was in the past now? He'd moved on, but it seemed her mother didn't feel Flora was allowed to. It just wasn't fair. And as for that crass comment about a child who'd lost her mother, and whose father was managing so brilliantly — oh, it was just too much.

She dashed away tears while negotiating the road to the main highway. She wouldn't allow her mother's thoughtless comments to spoil her day. But how could someone as kind and generous as her mum make such a hurtful remark?

She obviously has no idea how far Jack and I have come over these last months. Flora knew this was her own fault. She hadn't confessed her crush on an attractive male passenger, of course she hadn't. No one wanted to sound like a lovesick adolescent. But that crush had developed into liking and love — a love she knew was deep enough to last forever. How would her mother react to that?

Flora pulled into the station car park with minutes to spare. She needed to put money into the ticket machine, and it took a while to swallow the coins before disgorging a ticket. Flora dashed back to her car and stuck the ticket inside the windscreen. She hitched her bag on her shoulder and ran towards the steps leading to the bridge, her staff pass in her jacket pocket.

The train was standing beside the platform, several of its doors gaping wide. Flora made for the nearest one. She dropped into a window seat and rested her head against its back, briefly closing her eyes and thanking her lucky stars not to have been left behind on the platform.

'Hey, that was a narrow squeak!'

Flora groaned inwardly and opened her eyes with reluctance.

'We must stop meeting like this.' The guard's eyes were admiring.

'Hello, Gareth.' Flora smiled politely.

'*Bore da*, Flora.' He loved to show off his meagre command of the Welsh language, fully aware her knowledge of it was even scantier than his. 'Where are we off to, then?'

She produced her staff pass. He

waved it away. 'Off somewhere interesting?'

'Roseland Manor. Do you know it?'

'My folks go there sometimes for lunch. Isn't it a bit, well, fuddy-duddy for you?'

'Not at all; I love old houses. They often have fascinating histories.'

'So, are you going there on your own, then? What a shame.'

'I'm meeting a friend. Now, I'd better not hold you up any longer.' Surely he'd take the hint?

'Anyone I know?'

'I doubt it.'

'All dressed up and pretty in pink. Surely this isn't a date? Nah, it can't be. What kind of guy takes a girl to a stately home? Unless you're dating a geriatric.' Gareth chuckled at his own joke.

Flora raised her eyebrows but didn't allow him the satisfaction of an answer.

'Suit yourself, then.'

The guard set off down the train. 'How are you this morning then, sir?'

He was smiling down at an elderly gentleman wearing a summer suit and panama hat. 'Off to the cricket, I bet, you lucky fellow.'

Gareth had a lot going for him. Passengers enjoyed a chat when a train conductor could spare the time, but she'd been a bit fazed to see him this morning, especially after that comment of her mother's. Why, oh why, couldn't people mind their own business?

She gazed out at the passing landscape. There was the little grey church, looking dilapidated as usual but still standing bravely, looking out towards the estuary in the distance. Tip-tilted tombstones, some probably so ancient they'd seen out the last two centuries. She wished she could find the time to research it. There was so much history along this railway line, and she didn't even know when the track had first been laid. She'd try to remember to ask her father if he knew.

Soon after the next stop, the train

passed a large country hotel, set in well-manicured gardens. Flora leaned forward, noting the green-and-white-striped marquee and the hotel staff buzzing like bees between tent and hotel, doubtless preparing for a Saturday wedding. She wondered where Jack had got married. How strange if he and Charlotte had enjoyed their wedding reception at the lovely hotel she'd admired so many times when passing. No way did she intend asking him, as it would be a tactless thing to do. And part of her felt a tiny bit jealous of the happiness he'd shared with his late wife. How awful was that? What sort of a person was she?

She put all such thoughts from her mind and concentrated on the moment. It felt strange, relaxing and looking out of the window rather than charging up and down the train as she did when working. She would make the most of this free time, and with any luck, Gareth would be too busy to come back and shatter her peace.

'I hope you have a peaceful day, Clare.'

'You are joking!' But his sister-in-law grinned at him after giving Ellie a hug.

Jack and Clare watched Ellie and her older cousin hurry off, hand in hand, to play together.

'They can play this morning, we'll all have a picnic under the Faraway Tree at lunchtime, then I'll sit them down to watch *Frozen* for the ninety-ninth time.'

'Even I've been made to watch that particular film.' Jack looked at Ellie's case. 'Should I carry that upstairs?'

'No, you get off. You're meeting the train, aren't you?'

'Yes, but there's plenty of time. Ellie's been ready since at least five a.m.'

'Then you've time for a coffee?'

'I can always make time for a coffee.' Jack followed Clare through to the streamlined kitchen that he thought was as different from her parents' ramshackle one as it could possibly be. But the atmosphere was equally welcoming.

'Can I smell baking?'

'Cupcakes. I'll try to keep the girls from overloading them with sprinkles, and we'll save you one for tomorrow.'

'I'll look forward to it.' He pulled out a stool from the breakfast bar and perched on it while Clare filled the kettle and spooned ground coffee into a cafetière. 'OK. She's lovely, and when you meet, I very much hope you'll like her.'

Clare turned round. 'How did you know what I was going to ask you?'

He shrugged. 'It was the elephant in the room. You're bound to be curious. All of you.'

'I take it you haven't introduced your young lady to Mum and Dad yet?'

'Hardly! We haven't been seeing one another that long.' He corrected himself. 'Apart from nods and hellos on the train over the last months.'

'So I gather. Hang on — let me finish this. It won't take long to brew.'

Jack stared out at the vegetable

garden beyond the kitchen window.

'OK. So her name is Flora and she's a train conductor. She must work weird hours?'

'Not really. Her shifts vary, but she does get a weekend off from time to time.'

'Like this one! Where are you taking her?'

'We both like old houses and castles. Seeing the weather forecast, I thought we should grab the chance to visit Roseland Manor. The gardens look terrific on their website.'

'I went there with the school ages ago. You must let me know if it's somewhere the girls might like to go. It's probably changed a lot since I visited.'

'Yep.' Jack grinned. 'I hear they have electricity and running water now.'

She flipped a tea towel at him, opened the oven and took out a baking tray. 'You know what I mean. Everywhere has a shop, and at least a café. If there's a play area, the girls would love that too.'

She set the hot cakes down on top of the oven and began flipping them onto a cooling rack.

'Shall I pour the coffee while you sort those?'

'OK. Tell you what would be really good . . . '

Jack picked up the cafetière. 'What's that?'

'To see what Flora looks like. Do you have a photo?'

He frowned. 'Goodness, no, it never occurred to me. I'm — I'm hopeless at all this stuff, aren't I?'

Clare clasped her hands in front of her. 'You're doing brilliantly — we all think so. And we know it's time you got sorted out with someone lovely. It'll be good for you and good for Ellie, Jack.'

He nodded. 'I know. Flora's lovely, all right. But the daft thing is, Clare, I think Charlotte would have got on wonderfully with her. Flora's much quieter, but deep down that sister of yours was quite a private person, wasn't she?'

'Indeed she was.' Clare joined him at the breakfast bar. 'So take a photograph of Flora today, and when you come for Ellie tomorrow morning, I can sneak a look!'

'I can't do those selfie things.'

'Phone. Flora. Aim. Shoot! You can do it, Jack. I have faith in you.'

'I'll tell her how you treat me, then watch out!'

'And I'll tell you, Jack Slater, it's fantastic to see a sparkle back in your blue eyes. If that's down to Flora, she gets my vote any day.'

★　★　★

Jack, arriving on the station platform, thought on how his life seemed defined by train timetables. At least he *had* a life again, outside of the one revolving around his little daughter. He'd felt overwhelmed with the tide of love and protectiveness that hit him the day he watched Ellie's arrival into the world. Charlotte had dealt with childbirth as calmly as she dealt with most life events, but their daughter's birth had been the biggest, most wonderful, utterly awesome one of all. The love he shared with Ellie's mum would never die.

But people didn't need to remind him, even though they treated him with consideration, how important it was for him to love again. And as he watched the train snaking along the track, pulling into the little station, he suddenly couldn't wait to see Flora. He'd walked to the far end of the platform, lost in his memories. Now he realised the train, consisting of three coaches, had halted at the other end. He jogged back down the platform and there she was, jumping down from the last carriage.

'Hi,' he called.

She began jogging towards him. He held out his arms and she ran into them. He hugged her close, forgetting to feel embarrassed. Forgetting to look round to see if anyone was watching.

Forgetting everything but Flora and how much he'd looked forward to seeing her.

'Gosh,' she said, after he kissed her. 'I think I love you, Jack.'

The world swirled round him. 'Yes, Flora,' he said, 'I think I love you, too. For two fairly shy people, we're not doing so badly, are we?'

She laughed. 'You could say that.'

They walked hand in hand towards the exit, Flora asking him about Ellie, not sounding hesitant as she sometimes had before.

'I like that dress you're wearing,' he said. 'Those huge white spots on the pink — Ellie will want one just like it!'

'She shall have one,' Flora said. 'My mother made mine for me. When you feel the time's right, you could bring Ellie over for tea, and Mum will show her some patterns.'

Jack squeezed her hand. The train was about to pull away. He glanced back at it and his gaze met that of the guard, the only person on the platform, about to hop on board and close the door. Why the heck did the man look so belligerent? But he hadn't time to think about anything other than the hours together he and Flora were so anticipating.

'It's a twenty-minute drive, apparently,' Jack said, opening the passenger door for her.

'I want to take photos. As a keepsake.'

'I want to take a photograph of you,' he said.

Settling himself beside her, he noticed her pink cheeks and touched the one nearest with his forefinger. 'Darling Flora,' he said. 'Thank you for coming into my life.'

She leaned in and kissed him lightly on the lips. 'No, Jack, it's you I want to thank for coming into mine. And for giving me the chance to share a tiny bit of Ellie with you, if she'll allow it.'

'She'll adore you. I've dropped a hint now and again, but like you said, we'll know when it's the right time.'

Flora nodded. 'I hope so.'

'Now, over to the satnav. I'd sooner trust modern technology than my navigation through these country roads.'

★ ★ ★

As they drew closer, Flora noticed the brown historic building signs, reassuring them they were following the right route. When Jack drove through the entrance gate, there were several cars already in the car park, plus a coach bearing the name of a German tour operator.

'Roseland Manor's very popular with tourists from all over the world,' Jack said as they got out of the car. 'It's a well-preserved example of a Tudor manor house, and built in the latter part of the sixteenth century.' He glanced at Flora. 'What's so funny?'

'It's just that you sound like a guidebook! But keep going, Jack. It's interesting.'

'Ha! I learnt a lot from the website. The original family, as you'd expect were wealthy and titled. When the Civil War broke out in 1642, they were on the side of the Royalists.'

'Would they have had to defend the house?'

'I'm not sure, but I imagine having walls four feet thick would have made them feel secure.'

'As secure as anyone would feel with a war splitting the country.'

'True. Now, I'll get our tickets, and we can start our tour.'

Flora looked up at the big grey stone dwelling as she stood by the ticket office, and felt a little surge of excitement at the thought of the day ahead. When she'd visited castles or great houses with her mother or with the school, she'd always loved walking into a room and imagining a family from a long-gone era: sitting there, passing time, worrying about civil war, or looking forward to a party or a ball. How different life was nowadays.

Jack handed her a leaflet illustrating the house's layout, and also the various sections of its grounds. 'Where would you like to start?' he asked.

'Shall we follow our noses? Unless there's a recommended route.'

'I like your idea.'

'Before we begin, could I take your photo? They don't allow them to be taken in the house, and it's nice and sunny here but not too glary.' Flora took out her camera. 'You could stand on the front steps and look as if you live here.'

'I'll do my best, but I don't think funds will allow me to put Roseland Manor on my shopping list.' He moved across and made a face. 'How's that?'

'A smile would be better, my lord. I'll take a couple while I'm at it.'

'Maybe I'd better take a couple of you before we move on.' He moved to allow her to take his place. 'If I turn up to collect Ellie and I don't have a photo of you to show her aunt, I shall be in big trouble.'

'I'll do my best not to squint!'

They moved inside the house, and walked across the hallway where ancestral portraits lined the walls.

'Some of them look a bit forbidding,' Jack said.

'The children look as if they're on their best behaviour,' Flora was gazing up at the portrait of a small girl with black ringlets and solemn dark eyes. 'Goodness, I wonder who she grew up to marry. Maybe we'll see a portrait of her with children around her.'

Flora came to a standstill at the entrance to the big dining hall, her attention caught by a movement near the huge fireplace halfway down the room.

'That man could easily have stepped out of a history book,' she said. 'He's polishing those tiles as if his life depended on it.'

'We'll probably see quite a few servants around, dressed as they'd have been dressed back then. I thought you'd enjoy that.'

Flora nodded. 'It's a great idea. Are we allowed to ask them questions?'

'Oh, I think so.'

'Shall I ask him if they're expecting company?'

'Why not?'

15

Flora, Jack thought, seemed a little subdued on the drive back. He'd been thrilled by her enthusiasm about the stately home and the historical re-enactment, as the costumed actors allowed visitors a thrilling peep into the past by carrying out such roles as dairymaid, steward and under-cook. After they left the manor, Jack took the picturesque coast road, so the two of them walked hand in hand on the golden sands at low tide. Finally, they stopped off at a pub and sat in the garden with Ploughman's platters and long cool drinks; talking about their likes and dislikes: laughing, agreeing, and sometimes protesting. It had been a magical day for him — and, he hoped for Flora also.

'Are you all right?' Jack asked as they set off back to the station.

'Fine, thanks.'

'I mean really all right, not just trying to reassure me.' He glanced across, unsure as to her mood.

'I'm sorry. I didn't realise you were so tuned into my feelings.' Flora was twisting her fingers together.

'Well, that's a good sign, isn't it?'

'Of course! It's been an amazing day, and I — oh, I just feel sad it's coming to an end, I suppose. I enjoy my job, but my hours don't make things easy for us to meet.'

'We'll manage somehow, so don't fret. I'm sorry I can't see you tomorrow, but I've promised to take Ellie and her cousin swimming in the morning. Then it's lunch back at the ranch . . . '

'You don't need to apologise, Jack. You and Ellie need time together. Precious time. I'm being greedy.'

He felt a wave of tenderness. 'If it's any consolation, darling, I feel the same. Things will be easier when we can all three of us do things together. If that's all right with you, of course.'

She swallowed hard. 'I can't wait. And I'm sorry to be silly. I'm still thinking about the manor house and all we saw.'

'You're not being silly.' He reached for her hand.

'At the manor house, I felt almost as though we were time travellers from the future. Imagine life as a servant back in the reign of Charles I, having to get up before the dawn chorus and toil away at all those domestic tasks while the family were still slumbering sweetly.'

'They didn't know any different in those days. The servants knew their place and the family members knew theirs.'

'I'd have been a lowly maid, I imagine.'

'No, definitely a lady's maid, while I'd have been mucking out the stables and worshipping you from afar.'

They exchanged glances and laughed.

'I doubt we'd have ever had a lunch like the one we had today. It was absolutely delicious.' Flora glanced sideways again. 'And now I know you have a weakness for chocolate, just as I do.'

'That pudding was tip-top, but it's a good job we did a lot of walking afterwards.'

'Thank you for a wonderful day, Jack.'

'My pleasure — it takes two, you know.' He squeezed her hand before moving his to change gear. 'I wish it could go on longer, but — well, maybe next time we could work something out.'

'Now I have my own car, we could meet somewhere halfway next time.'

'That sounds good. Do you want to fix a date now, or will you let me know what suits you?'

'I can make any evening next week as I'm on the early service.'

'You won't want too late a night, though? You'll be signing on before seven a.m.'

'It's not so bad these summer mornings.'

'Come to think of it, I have an estate agent ringing on Monday to confirm a viewing time, so shall we say we'll meet at Ashfield as early in the week as possible?'

'Lovely.' Flora checked her watch. 'We're fine for time.'

'Just as well, as I think the nine-thirty's the last one, isn't it?'

'Yes, it'd be a bit awkward if I missed it.'

'I'd have to drive you back.' He shot her a mischievous glance. 'Not a bad idea, in fact — it'd give us more time together.'

'Jack Slater, keep your eyes on the road and behave!'

He knew she was scolding him good-humouredly but all he could think about was whether she'd object to him giving her a proper goodnight kiss before she got out of the car. They weren't far away from the station, and soon Jack was dropping her off again and saying goodbye. He cut the engine and turned to her.

'I feel almost as though we're acting in *Brief Encounter* but without the steam trains!' Flora turned to face him.

'I hope we're not,' Jack said. 'My mother used to like that film, and from what I can remember, the couple were old enough to have known better.'

'My mum has very strict ideas, but they didn't stop her from enjoying it!'

'I must speak sternly to her when we meet.'

'Good luck with that.'

He laughed. Moved a little closer. 'At least we don't gaze soulfully at one another across a pot of tea and two buttered scones.'

'Not yet, but it sounds fun.'

He put his arms around her and she nestled against his chest, then tilted her chin.

'Flora . . . '

'Yes, Jack . . . ?'

'Oh, heck!' At last his lips met hers, and to his overwhelming relief, their kiss seemed to be the most natural thing in the world.

Flora remained in her own private kingdom while the train rattled along the track towards her home station. Since her initial attraction to the anonymous Mr Gorgeous, she'd progressed to being one half of a couple, and was more in love with him than ever. He'd called her *darling*. And that first, wonderful kiss lasted so long, her head was whirling when it came to an end. Jack had smiled shyly at her and lifted his hand to stroke a lock of hair away from her face.

'I love you,' he'd whispered. 'I want you to know I love you because you're unique and you're beautiful and you're my Flora, and no way are you a replacement. I think it's important you know that.'

She'd struggled to reply, so overwhelmed did she feel. 'Thank you,' she said, touched that he'd maybe sensed he should smooth away any doubts over living up to his first love.

'You mean so much to me,' she murmured, unable to prevent a tear or two from trickling down her cheeks.

'And you to me. Hey, I hope these mean joy,' Jack said, gently using his thumbs to brush away her teardrops.

So engrossed were the two with one another, in the end she'd leapt from the car and run towards the station, clutching Jack's hand until the pair, now in fits of laughter, managed to arrive on the platform only moments before the driver halted the train. The guard jumped out, noticed a familiar face and gave Flora a friendly wave.

'I'll ring you soon,' Jack called as she boarded. She sank into a seat and watched him standing there until the train set off and she could no longer see him through her window.

She exchanged a few words with the guard, a senior employee who had helped train Trudy in her early days with the company. Before moving on, he asked whether Flora had seen her mentor lately, and this triggered thoughts of the coming party. Jack hadn't mentioned it, and while floating on her personal pink cloud of happiness, she'd forgotten to ask if she could be left off the schedule for that particular date. She'd have to send an email as soon as possible and hope for the best. Trudy hadn't been in touch for a while, so Flora resolved to make that two emails on her to-do list.

Meanwhile, it was great to reach the station and go straight to her own car, without the need to disturb her father's evening.

* * *

'So, when do we get to meet Flora? I hope you remembered to take her photo!'

When Jack arrived on the doorstep next morning, his sister-in-law had the two girls' swimming kit plus towels rolled up and packed in a sports bag.

'And good morning to you too, Clare! I'm early, I think?'

'You are. Well done.'

'You'll be pleased to hear I managed to take a couple of photos. But as for meeting Flora, I think I need to sort your mum and dad out first, don't you? Possibly at home with Ellie there, d'you think?'

'Ah, yes, of course. Trust me, jumping in with both feet. I'm sorry, Jack.'

He shrugged. 'I wondered about meeting somewhere neutral, but would that make it more of a big deal for Ellie?'

'Maybe. Familiar surroundings would probably be best. They have at least seen one another before, haven't they?'

'Only fleetingly, and I'm sure Ellie's forgotten Flora by now, but it's not worth worrying about until they meet properly.'

'How much have you said?'

Jack took out his phone and scrolled to the previous day's photo shoot. He handed the phone to Clare. 'Not much really, except to say that I've made a new friend.' He grinned. 'Ellie seemed much more interested in Flora's job than in the fact that Daddy had a girlfriend.'

Clare was studying Flora's photographs. 'She looks great — bit of a shock seeing her brown hair, though. For some reason I thought she'd be blonde, but she's an attractive girl.' She looked up. 'Um, her job could be a good icebreaker when she meets Ellie.'

'Good thinking. I have a house to view tomorrow, but I'll speak to Flora soon and set up a date for her to come over, as long as it's OK with Megan and Robbie.'

Jack's sister-in-law was studying Flora's photographs again. 'She looks so young.'

'Is that a criticism? I'm not that old, you know!'

'Of course you're not, but Flora's twenty-three to your thirty.' She hesitated.

'And Charlotte was eighteen months older than me. It's no big deal, Clare.'

'I'm sorry — I shouldn't have said anything.'

'I'm sorry too. I'm a bit sensitive — and, if I'm honest, a little nervous about Flora's reactions as well as Ellie's.'

Clare reached up to give him a hug. 'We're all on your side, Jack. I hope you realise that.'

'Certainly do! Now, do you want to give the mermaids a call? And can I trust them to cope in the ladies' changing room?'

'I have a couple of friends we always see at the Sunday morning session, and I've told them you're bringing the girls today. So there'll be someone looking out for them and making sure their stuff gets safely into the locker. And out again!'

'You're a star,' he said. 'Now, if I could have my phone back, please?'

16

Flora hurried along the platform towards the door marked Staff Only, trying to catch up with her friend. 'Trudy!'

Trudy stopped and turned around, her face brightening as she saw who was behind her. 'Hello, stranger, I was hoping you'd get my email in time.'

'Yes, thank you. So we can have a chat over lunch?'

Trudy pushed open the door. 'Or brunch, or whatever. I'm starving!'

Flora followed her to the counter. Once they sat down with their drinks, waiting for their food to arrive, Trudy looked sternly across.

'You've kept that a secret!'

'Kept what?'

'Might it be your romance with Jack Slater? Ring any bells?'

Flora felt heat flood her cheeks.

'Gosh, I'm sorry, Trudy. To be honest, I really didn't believe he could feel the same about me as I do about him. I didn't want to say anything until we'd allowed ourselves time to feel quite sure about each other.'

'I understand, and I'm very pleased for you and for Jack, of course, although I haven't met him.'

'He thinks you might recognise each other when you come face to face.'

'It's possible. But the main thing is, you look so happy. And he does too, according to my husband.' She stirred her tea. 'You can stop blushing now.'

Flora shook her head. 'I wish. The only consolation is that Jack likes to see me blush — weird though that might seem.'

'It's part of you, so don't knock it.' Trudy sat back as their food arrived.

'Has Jack said anything to your husband?' Flora took a slice of toast.

'They had a bite to eat together the other day; and Jack, although he took a while to get round to it, confessed he'd lost his heart to a wonderful girl called Flora.' Trudy looked her in the eye. 'Apparently, you were on his mind for ages, until one day he found the courage to approach you and take it from there. Is that right?'

'I think that sounds about right. I was travelling as a passenger that day, and there was a delay which actually did us a favour.' She explained how things had progressed after that.

'I'm so pleased you found each other. It's so romantic, meeting on a train! And you can come to the party as a couple now, can't you?'

'I hope so. Jack hasn't said anything, but he has a lot on his mind, what with us getting together just as he's beginning his house-hunting.'

'He's moving? Are you involved?'

'Goodness, I'm not moving in with him, if that's what you mean. I think my mother would have forty fits. But he wants me to go with him when he finds somewhere he really likes, and decides to view it a second time.' She bit her lip.

'Provided it fits with my work schedule, of course.'

'Hmm. If that's what he's suggesting, I'd say it was highly significant.'

'Well, it's a big decision, I imagine. He obviously wants to remain in the area, not only because of his job but for Ellie's sake, and for her grandparents too. It seems as if he's a good father.'

'I can understand him longing for his own place again, but won't he find it hard, sorting out child-minding and doing all the chores once he hasn't got his in-laws standing by?'

'He must've thought of all that, Trudy. Ellie's at primary school, and she has a cousin not much older, so I imagine that's part of the plan. He's not short of child-minding offers.'

Trudy took a deep breath. 'You don't think — gosh, I'm sorry if I'm speaking out of turn, but . . . might meeting you have led to him regarding you as a potential mum for Ellie?'

Flora felt as though a huge cold hand was gripping her, and she shivered instinctively. Surely Jack had been sincere when he revealed his feelings? She hadn't even met his daughter properly yet. What if Ellie didn't take to her? How would Jack cope with that? How would she herself feel, knowing her shiny new romance might end in tears because a six-year-old child held the balance of power?

'Oh heck, I'm so sorry.' Trudy, her face troubled, put down her fork. 'That didn't come out right at all, did it? I meant to say, it would be a triple bonus for you all if you and Jack were to settle down together. He's obviously head over heels — as you are, Flora.'

'It's early days. We need to spend more time learning about one another before we go any further.'

'I'm so looking forward to meeting him. Now, tell me what you're wearing to the party.'

But Flora didn't quite succeed in banishing gloomy thoughts from her mind. And niggling little doubts over whether she could cope with a relationship already loaded with emotional baggage lingered and refused to go away.

* * *

Jack viewed four houses before he knew he wanted to visit two of them a second time. He decided to ring Flora that evening, knowing she'd be at home, or at least wouldn't be working. He didn't intend on taking her for granted, but life was hectic for both of them. Each had different demands on their time, and sometimes he wished he could just stop the carousel from revolving: jump off, holding Ellie's hand on one side and Flora's on the other, and fly away to some sunny, tranquil paradise where they could get to know one another away from the pressures of the daily routine. That wasn't going to happen any day soon.

Flora answered her phone on the second ring.

The moment he heard her voice, he couldn't stop himself from smiling. 'Hello, gorgeous girl!'

'How are you, Jack?'

Something wasn't quite right. He responded, then asked, 'How are you, Flora? I hope you didn't think I was avoiding contacting you. It's been busy at work, several people on holiday, then the house hunting ... ' His voice trailed off.

'No, I understand. But, Jack, a friend has called round to see me. Could I call you back?'

'Of course,' he said. 'I'm ringing on the landline. Lack of a signal's one thing I shan't miss when we move out.'

'I'll ring you later, then.' She closed the call.

He blinked hard. Flora was normally chatty, sounding delighted to hear from him and asking after Ellie. This evening, though unknowingly he'd rung at an awkward time, she seemed a little distant.

He fancied taking a stroll. Near the

entrance to the yard, there was a path leading through woodland and on to a large lake. But he daren't risk missing her call. He couldn't remember at which point of the walk he might stop receiving even a weak signal, and at the moment he didn't fancy chancing his luck. He decided to go upstairs, firstly putting his head round the kitchen door to tell Megan he was expecting a call and would be in his room.

'I'll bring the phone upstairs, that way I won't have to shout to you and risk waking Ellie,' she said.

Upstairs, he opened his laptop and called up the estate agent's website, intent on taking another look at the houses he'd arranged to view. He hoped Flora could meet him. If not, he was big enough and ugly enough to make his own decision — though, more and more, he felt convinced he wanted her to be part of his new life. But was she prepared to become Ellie's stepmother? He daren't even consider how he'd feel, should she refuse. It was a lot to ask, and of course they both still needed time. But, if he knew she liked the look of either of his two selected houses, he'd find it a tremendous help . . . and maybe a good omen for the future.

*   *   *

She'd told a white lie. Not a horrendous porky pie, but serious enough to make her squirm. She wasn't entertaining anybody when Jack rang. Her mum was chatting to the mother of one of Flora's old school friends in the sitting room, and Flora was on her way to the kitchen to make a pot of tea when her phone chimed. Now she stood, arranging homemade flapjacks on a plate and waiting for the kettle to boil. Being involved with humdrum tasks was often helpful when mulling over a momentous decision.

She hadn't found much time to think while continuing her working day. Nor did she think Trudy was being deliberately uncaring or hurtful by bringing up a fear Flora had so far managed to keep to herself. If you fell in love with a widower who had a young child, it stood to reason that child must be his main priority. She already knew that, of course. So why did hearing her friend voice the possibility spook Flora so badly that she wondered whether her own feelings were as sincere as they should be?

She poured water into the teapot and carried the tray into the sitting room. She set the tea things on the coffee table and straightened up.

'Not joining us, love?' Her mum had spotted the tray was set for two.

'No, I'm fine, thanks. I have to make a phone call so I'll leave you both to it.'

'All right, my dear, we'll see you later then.'

Flora went straight upstairs and sat down on her bed. Her father was pottering in his shed, probably listening to the radio, and pleased he wasn't stuck in the sitting room having to be polite. She wondered whether to go and talk to him, take him a cuppa, and see what he made of her dilemma. Then it dawned on her. She knew how she must proceed. Waiting any longer would only prolong the agony. Before she could change her mind, she called up Jack's number. She thought the person who answered must be Ellie's grandma, and straightaway she asked if she could speak to Jack.

'He's upstairs, Flora. Hang on while I hand over the phone.'

Flora waited. And when Jack greeted her, he sounded so eager and pleased to hear from her, she felt her doubts melt away like chocolate left to soften on a saucer beside a glowing fire. But the time had come to speak up.

'I'm sorry about earlier,' she said. 'I'm on my own now, and I have something I need to talk to you about.'

17

'Oh dear, should I be worried?' Jack sounded hesitant.

'No, it's only that I know you have lots on your mind, but I really would like to meet Ellie as soon as it can be arranged.' Her words came tumbling out. She needed to know where she stood. Yes, on the surface everything might seem to be sunshine and roses regarding Jack and herself, but there was one very important little person involved in this, and she couldn't ignore Ellie any longer.

'It sounds as though you've been thinking things through,' Jack said.

'Yes, I have. I know you felt we should take our time, but it's not as simple as that. Neither of us works routine hours, so it'll probably take a while to fix a convenient time and place.'

'Fair enough,' Jack said. 'But I can't decide whether it would be best to meet somewhere like a teashop, or whether you'd prefer coming here. How would you feel about that, Flora? You and Ellie are the important ones.'

She chuckled. 'Of course we are!'

'I think it's important for everyone to feel relaxed. It might be a bit overwhelming for you to meet my daughter and my in-laws all at the same time.'

'I imagine Ellie enjoys going out and about with you?'

'You bet!'

'So, how about visiting a country park or wildlife centre, maybe? I could meet you two there, and we could look round and concentrate on the animals rather than sit at a table trying to think up things to say.'

'I like the sound of that,' Jack said. 'According to the local news, the wildlife centre where I took Ellie that day you rescued her teddy bear has some new animals, including babies.

What do you think?'

'It sounds perfect. You could text me some dates?'

'Weekends only?'

'With the light evenings, we could maybe fit in a visit one afternoon after Ellie finishes school. A couple of hours would probably be enough for her.'

'She does get tired some days,' Jack said. 'I'd hate it if she was grumpy!'

'I'm willing to take the chance. We all have off days.'

'Then let's go for it. I'll check my diary and let you know.'

'I can sometimes swap shifts. I'm sure we can work something out.'

'You sound excited!'

'I am,' she said. 'Who's more important — Ellie, or you and me?'

He hesitated. 'I hope you know by now how much you mean to me, but Ellie's just a child, darling.'

'Precisely,' Flora said. 'I love you very much, but if our relationship is to continue, your daughter must be an important part of it.'

There was a pause. Flora waited and wondered.

'To be honest, I've been worrying about the situation,' Jack said at last. 'There was always a danger you might think I was looking for a replacement mother for Ellie, and now I know that's simply not true. And the more I get to know you, the more I want to be with you.'

'Me too,' Flora said.

★　★　★

Four days later, Flora drove into the car park of the wildlife centre she hadn't visited since she was eleven years old. She got out of her car, and straight away heard Jack calling her name. She zapped her key to lock her vehicle and walked to meet him, knowing he'd told Ellie he wanted her to meet a good friend of his.

He stood hand in hand with his daughter. Ellie, her blonde curls tamed with a red ribbon, wore her school uniform of white shirt and red skirt.

'Hi Flora,' Jack greeted her, and released his daughter's hand to give her a hug. Flora couldn't help but notice Ellie's guarded expression, so returned the hug, then turned to the child who'd grabbed her daddy's hand again.

'It's lovely to meet you, Ellie. You look so smart in your uniform. Have you had a good day?'

'Yes, thank you,' she said.

'I've bought our tickets,' Jack said. 'What do you young ladies think we should see first?'

'You choose, Ellie,' Flora said.

'Dinosaurs!'

'Oh dear, I think they're all asleep this afternoon,' Flora said. 'How about meerkats or lemurs?'

'Both! Can we, please, Daddy?'

'Come on, then.'

They set off, following the signs, Ellie and Jack hand in hand, and Flora unsure whether to walk beside Jack or the little girl. She opted for Jack and bided her time. He gave her a swift smile, as if to say *Slowly does it*, and asked whether she remembered much about her first visit to the park.

'It was years ago, and they hadn't been open long. My most vivid memory is of the big slide in the play area. But I can remember there were plenty of farm animals and their young. I'm sure there was nothing more exotic than a duckling in those days.'

As they spotted the meerkat enclosure in the distance, Ellie let go of her father's hand and ran on ahead.

'That's a good sign,' Jack said, taking hold of Flora's hand. 'When we're on our own, she normally sticks to my side like glue.'

'Like you said, let's take it nice and steady.'

And when they moved on to watch the lemurs, Ellie was quick to question. 'Why are you holding the lady's hand, Daddy? Are you afraid she'll get lost?'

Flora hid a smile.

'I'm holding Flora's hand because I'm fond of her, sweetheart.'

Ellie said nothing and took hold of her daddy's free hand. But when they were ready to move on from the lemurs and inspect the penguin colony, Ellie stood, head to one side, as if considering her options.

Flora hadn't expected to feel such a surge of delight when the little girl clasped her hand, and with the other one held on to her father's. She didn't know whether Ellie wanted to separate Daddy's new friend from him, or whether the move was entirely innocent. No doubt time would tell; but for now, Flora wasn't complaining.

★ ★ ★

Nor did she complain when she met Jack a few stops down her usual line and viewed a house with him. The property, situated on a small residential estate, looked out on to farming land at the rear. It wasn't far from the railway station, and was only three miles from Jack's sister-in-law's house.

He pulled up outside and cut the motor.

'This is it. Number 21. We're a little early, so the agent hasn't arrived yet.'

'It looks lovely, even on a rainy afternoon,' Flora said.

'There's a fabulous view through the windows at the back, but it's a bit too murky out there today.' He turned to her and took her hands in his. 'Lovely Flora, I do hope you like this house.'

'You sounded very enthusiastic on the phone,' she said. 'I expect I'll like it if you do.'

'I'd rather you gave me an honest opinion, darling.' He scrabbled in the glove compartment and produced a set of particulars.

'Thanks, but it's not up to me, Jack. You're the one doing the buying. You and Ellie will be the ones living in it.' She felt genuinely puzzled that he should consider her opinion important.

Jack sucked in his breath. 'Flora — I've been meaning to say this to you for a while now . . . ' He paused as a car manoeuvred its way between his vehicle and the one parked a little further down. 'Too late; that's the estate agent.'

'What did you want to say?'

'It — it doesn't matter now. I'll tell you later.'

They got out of the car. Jack greeted the woman wearing a smart navy blue suit, and introduced Flora as a friend helping him decide.

The estate agent gave her what Flora considered a very searching look before preceding them up the drive and unlocking the front door.

They walked into a small hallway, with a modern staircase and a single door to their left.

'Reception room number one,' announced the agent. Flora followed her into a light, airy space, looking out on the close and with an archway leading to a dining area.

'Open-plan, but you can be separate,' said Flora, walking through.

'And here's the kitchen.' The estate agent opened another door.

'This is lovely,' said Flora, eyeing the modern range cooker and the slate worktops. There was also a small breakfast bar and plenty of cupboard space.

They walked out into a passage with a downstairs cloakroom one side. 'Small, but perfectly formed,' Flora announced.

'Very useful,' Jack agreed.

'You'll see the utility room has a sink, plus space for all the usual things.'

Flora, trying to be helpful and practical, asked whether the washing machine was staying or going.

'Going, definitely,' the agent said. 'I believe it states as much on the particulars.'

'Whoops!' Flora felt slightly foolish, but Jack was taking no notice.

'I don't think we'll go outside in this weather,' he said. 'The garden's perfect for us as it's not too large. But I reckon that dining room needs a conservatory extension, to take full advantage of that view.'

Flora noticed the agent's eyes gleam. 'I imagine that would be no problem?' she asked.

'Not at all,' said the agent. 'The property next door has had a conservatory added since we sold it three years ago.'

The upstairs tour showed three bedrooms, the master bedroom complete with en-suite facilities. The two other bedrooms were smaller, but the one decorated in pink obviously belonging to a little girl. Flora smiled as she took in the framed print of a scene from the film *Frozen*, and noticed the pink-and-purple butterfly pattern on the thick white curtains.

Back downstairs, the agent walked into the kitchen to answer a call on her mobile phone, and Jack looked at Flora. 'So, what do you think?'

'I like the house very much. I think it's perfect for you and Ellie, both because of its location and because it has a friendly feel. Why is it on the market?'

'The owners are relocating. Another baby on the way, and a job move, so they're anxious to get cracking.' He hesitated. 'If you're sure you like this one, I'm going to make an offer.'

'I prefer this to the one you showed me last week, although that had more ground.'

'Yep,' he said. 'But this one's in the better location as far as we three are concerned.'

Flora felt as though the world suddenly tilted.

Jack met her gaze. 'I'm sorry, darling. I meant to talk to you properly, not blurt it out without warning. Look, I daren't risk our friendly agent walking in on us, so let's go and find somewhere to park up and I'll explain what's on my mind.'

18

Jack drove slowly down the road leading to the local marina, and slotted his car into the nearest space. He cut the engine and turned to Flora.

'See that view? Makes me want to grab a little sailing boat so I can cast off and sail into the sunset with you.'

She chuckled. 'I'm a terrible sailor; you'd soon regret it if I joined your crew.'

'Never!'

'Jack, why don't you stop beating about the bush and tell me what's on your mind?'

He gripped the steering wheel and stared straight ahead. 'I suppose I'm afraid you won't agree to my suggestion.'

'Well, you'll never know unless you ask.' She turned her head to hide her amusement. He so often reminded her of the way she dealt with life.

'I think what I'm about to say has been simmering away inside me for months now, Flora. When I first saw you on the train, I must admit I didn't act as if I was pleased to make your acquaintance.'

'You hardly had time.'

'Maybe not, but your sparkling green eyes and pretty hair caught my attention. I haven't told you before how I'd been sneaking little glances at you for a while before Ellie lost her teddy bear.'

'Well, I was on my way to visit my aunt, and I also had a lot on my mind.' One day, maybe she'd confess how she'd given him the nickname of Mr Gorgeous.

'I found it difficult to put you out of my thoughts. So, that time I realised the train manager was the same girl I'd admired, I couldn't believe my luck. But I soon decided you were bound to have a boyfriend or husband. I thought someone as attractive as you couldn't possibly be unattached.'

'You found out differently,' she said gently, a tiny smile trembling on her lips.

'And I thank my lucky stars I did, my darling.' He drew her to him and Flora snuggled against his chest. She loved the way she felt when in the haven of his arms. Loved the way the warmth of his skin brought out the fresh tang of his lemony shaving lotion. Loved to hear his voice.

'It's taken me a while to get to this point.' Jack said. 'But I've definitely decided to make an offer on that house we just viewed.'

'Great,' Flora said. 'You know I'll do everything I can to lend a hand when it comes to moving day, whether it's that house or some other one. I know your mum-in-law and sister-in-law will look out for you but I'd be thrilled to help make the house into a home for you both.'

'Thank you very much, but I'd prefer it to be a home for the three of us.'

She froze. He didn't seem to notice.

'I'm well aware this isn't the right time to bring up the matter, and I realise the need to be patient. I haven't even met your parents yet, and nor have you met Megan and Robbie. These things are important and can't be rushed.'

'It . . . it hasn't been easy, finding time to arrange visits. My work schedule doesn't help.'

'And you know I try to see as much of Ellie as I possibly can. If we could all live together in one place, life would be so much easier, don't you think?'

'I — I don't quite know what to think.' Flora felt the first telltale surge of heat flood her cheeks. She hadn't expected him to be quite so blatant! He wanted her to move in with him and his daughter. Her mother and father would certainly disapprove, and nor would they understand. Even though their daughter was over the age of twenty-one, she couldn't fly in the face of their traditional values.

Anyway, what kind of a girl did Jack

think she was? The two of them had so often discussed and agreed the way they felt about many aspects of modern life. They'd even decided they should really have been born in a former era. Now he was making a daring suggestion, one she'd never dreamt she might hear from him.

She stopped looking at her hands and glanced sideways at the man beside her. He was bent over the steering wheel, his face hidden by his hands, and he was making the strangest of sounds. Either he was crying or he was choking. Surely he couldn't be laughing?

'Jack? Whatever's the matter?'

He uncovered his face and turned towards her, reaching for her hands. 'I knew I'd make a mess of this. Oh, sweetheart, your face was a picture, and no wonder. I'm mortified! Of course I wouldn't dream of asking you to move in with me without our being married. But, because of the reasons I've just mentioned, I shouldn't and don't intend to ask you the most important question a man can ask the woman he loves. Not yet, anyway.'

Relief and surprise whooshed through her body, making her feel quivery and slightly tearful. 'I think I'm having a fit of the vapours,' she said.

He hugged her to him again. 'I'm sorry if I upset you.' He kissed the top of her head. 'You have time to think how you really feel about a future together. And if I pass muster with your parents — '

'They will like you,' she said. 'And if Megan and Robbie approve of me . . . '

'No question about it! I told you how Ellie's been singing your praises.'

'I don't know whether to laugh or cry,' Flora said.

'Then why not kiss me?'

So she did.

* * *

Flora was working the early shift on the morning of Trudy and Dan's anniversary party, much relieved to have the schedule back to normal after track repairs. She'd kept an appointment with her hairdresser, and hoped Jack would approve of this different look.

'Wow, you look fantastic!' Jack kissed her lightly on the lips when he met her later.

'Thank you, kind sir. You look very smart yourself.'

'Cheers. It's ages since I went to a party. They're not really my scene,' he said, taking her overnight bag from her.

'Same here, so I'm glad I'll be walking in with you, rather than on my own, even if it's Trudy's place and not a big hotel.'

'So, you're staying the night with them?'

'Yes, Trudy asked me ages ago, when she told me to put the date in my diary.'

'I wish I could take you back with me afterwards,' Jack said. 'There's a guest room, but I can hardly turn up with you before you've met Megan and Robbie.' He unlocked his car.

'The good news is, I have tomorrow

free. Someone wanted to change shifts. I know it's short notice, but I could drive over if you'd like me to.'

'I think we could put up with that,' he teased, reaching for her hands. 'I can't help thinking it'd be easier for me to drive you home, so you'll be in the right place ready for tomorrow. Why don't you let me pick you up for lunch or tea, depending on what Megan says?'

'Are you sure?'

'Absolutely certain. By the way, you have one stray ringlet I'm longing to twirl round my finger. Is that permitted?'

'No way.' Flora made a face. 'The whole thing might collapse. It's only just long enough for me to be able to put it up.'

'You'll be the belle of the ball, but I love your hair whether it's up, down, or messy.'

'You say such lovely things,' she said. 'I do love you, Jack.'

'And I love you. Do we really have to go to this party?'

She sat up straight and frowned at him. 'Of course we do, you bad boy. Trudy's longing to meet you and she wants to introduce me to Dan. We don't have to stay too late, especially now you've offered to drive me home.'

'Thank goodness for small mercies.'

She watched him adjust his satnav. 'I think I know the way, but it's probably best to follow the directions.'

'Then off we go.'

'Is Ellie at home tonight? I'd like to see her again if tomorrow's convenient.'

'She's at home,' he said, changing gear. 'She has a new princess dress which she'd sleep in, given half a chance.'

Flora laughed. 'I can imagine. I used to love dressing up when I was a little girl, and I always used to think brides looked like princesses. Mum had to stop and let me watch if we ever passed a church on a Saturday afternoon when there was a wedding taking place.'

Suddenly stricken, she glanced swiftly at his profile. 'Jack, I'm sorry I said that. I guess you and Charlotte had a white wedding.'

'We did, but it's alright, Flora. You haven't trodden on my dreams. I think I must be a very lucky man, to have gained the love of someone as special as you.'

Flora looked out of the window and blinked hard. 'We're both lucky,' she said quietly. 'I wouldn't ever try to stop you remembering Ellie's mum. Your daughter is living proof of the happiness you both shared.'

They drove in silence for a while, until Jack said, 'I knew you were someone special, and I keep on being proved right.'

19

Trudy and Dan lived in a pretty white house, approached along a rough track. Jack parked his car on some nearby waste ground.

'I don't want to get blocked in and have to ask someone to move when we go home. Hopefully we can stagger this far.' He took Flora's hand and they headed towards the house, Flora picking her way carefully in her high heels.

'It sounds as if they're outside,' she said as they walked up the path. The front door stood open and faint sounds of music filtered from somewhere beyond.

'Hello?' Jack rang the doorbell.

She felt a shiver of anticipation. This was the first time she and Jack had gone out as a couple amongst friends and colleagues. She also wondered if Trudy would recognise him, or he her.

'How lovely to see you both!' Trudy, wearing white leggings beneath a white minidress patterned with tropical flowers, appeared and swiftly gave Flora a hug. 'You look gorgeous! Red really suits you, Flora.'

'Thank you, but you look beautiful too.' Flora handed Trudy a greetings card and a small gift wrapped in white tissue paper and tied with old-school brown string.

Trudy beamed. 'You really shouldn't have, but thank you so much, both of you. I'll open it later.' She turned her attention to Flora's escort.

'Hello, Trudy.' He held out his hand. 'I'm Jack, and I recognise you now. Thanks for inviting me.'

Trudy shook his hand. 'Yes, Jack, your face is familiar too. I'm so pleased to see you both. We're outside as it's such a beautiful evening, but all the food's inside ready for later. Come and say hi to Dan and the others.'

They followed their hostess across an

open-plan sitting- and dining-room, and through patio doors to a tiled terrace.

'This is great,' said Jack, looking round. 'Ah, I can see Dan over there.'

'Probably talking cricket as usual,' Trudy said. 'Now, what would you two like to drink? There's a non-alcoholic fruit punch, red or white wine, and beer on the go.'

After they each had a drink in hand, another train guard came up and greeted Flora. Dan spotted Jack, and having chatted to Flora, hauled him off to discuss the current local cricket situation. Flora was talking with her hostess again when she became aware of a man entering the room. He stopped to speak to someone, but came up to kiss his hostess's cheek and hand her a package.

'Hi, Gareth.' Trudy peered inside the gold foil bag. 'Ooh, thank you very much. I think I know what this is.'

'You can never have too much bubbly in the house.' Gareth smiled at Flora.

'Well, look who's here. The lady in red.'

Flora forced a smile and thanked her lucky stars she had Jack across the room. If she'd arrived alone, she had a feeling it might have been difficult to avoid spending time with Gareth.

To her dismay, Trudy was on the move again. 'I must put this somewhere safe and make sure everyone has something to drink. Beer, Gareth? I'll bring you one.' She hurried off.

'She looks radiant,' Flora said quickly. 'I've hardly spoken to Dan, but anyone can see how happy they are.'

Gareth raised an eyebrow. 'Well, they've survived ten years of marriage. That can't be bad.'

Flora felt irritated. 'I imagine they're looking forward to several more decades of togetherness.'

He shook his head. Took a quick swallow of his drink. 'That would drive me round the bend. Seeing the same face over the dinner table every night. I like a bit of variety in my relationships.' He smirked at Flora.

She sipped her fruit punch, so cool and delicious, and didn't quite know what to say. Gareth seemed to have shifted from friendly colleague to someone whose agenda she suspected. She'd lost that feeling of being comfortable with him, ever since he approached her at the station that time.

'You're quiet this evening. Where's the boyfriend?' He looked around.

Flora looked too, but there was no sign of Jack. She noticed one or two couples were dancing on the lawn. Gareth must have followed her gaze.

'At least someone's chosen some halfway decent music. Shall we have a dance?'

She had no wish to dance, but nor did she want to hold a conversation with him. Jack was probably chatting with someone else he knew from his office, so what was the harm in dancing, especially as the lawn was still half in sunshine? Trudy and Dan must have worked hard on the garden. They'd created a riot of colourful summer flowers and shrubs as well as planted a couple of saplings. She felt a little surge of happiness at the thought of planning a garden with Jack.

Flora put down her glass and followed her dance partner down the steps to the lawn. Another couple joined them just as the music changed from catchy and bouncy to sweet and soulful.

'Perfect timing,' he muttered in her ear as he took her in his arms. She tried to hold herself away from him, but he had a height advantage, and seemed determined to glue himself to her. She could hear Trudy's voice from inside the house, inviting people to help themselves to supper. Before she knew it, Gareth was steering her towards a shadowy corner beside a weeping willow tree. And she was becoming more and more convinced he'd been drinking before he arrived.

Flora stopped dancing and lowered both arms to her sides, expecting her partner to follow suit. But he pulled her beneath the leafy curtain of the willow tree, obviously intent upon kissing her.

'Hey, stop it. Please stop it at once!' She kept her voice low, at the same time trying to pull away, but not before he'd succeeding in planting a kiss on her mouth.

'That's better. What's a little kiss between friends? Now, how about relaxing, why can't you?'

'Flora, are you all right? Is there a problem?'

Thank goodness! To her relief, Jack pulled back the foliage and stood there, grim-faced.

'Hey, what's your problem mate? Flora and I were just enjoying getting to know each other better.' Gareth smirked at Flora.

Jack looked him in the eye. 'Flora's with me.'

She moved away from Gareth, who spread his hands. 'Well, there's a surprise,' he said. 'I assumed you were either not here, or none too fussed about taking care of your lady.'

Jack sucked in his breath. Flora saw he'd balled his hands into fists either side of his body.

She placed herself between the two men. 'Let's go back in. Trudy's serving supper now.' She looked at Gareth. 'I'm sorry if I gave you the impression I was here alone. Jack and I are, well, I suppose people would say we're an item.'

'Very much so,' Jack said, taking Flora's hand in his.

Gareth gave a short, sharp bark of laughter. 'Could've fooled me.' He winked at Jack. 'I'd keep an eye on her if I were you. She's a very friendly sort of girl . . . if you get my drift.'

He headed off towards the house.

Flora turned to Jack. 'I'm so sorry if I've upset you. Things moved quickly. Before I knew it, Gareth was grabbing me and pulling me out of everyone's view. I didn't think he meant anything bad.'

'You were quick enough to go and dance with him. I was on my way back to you when I saw you heading outside. Then someone stopped to talk to me and I didn't like to be rude.' His voice tailed off and he sighed, letting go of her hand. 'I know I'm not a very exciting person, Flora. It's not too late to change your mind about me, you know.'

She gazed at him, devastated by his bitter words. Fearing she might burst into tears, she swallowed a sob and took off back to the house.

'Flora, wait! Let's not fight over this. I didn't mean . . . ' His voice tailed off again. She didn't look back.

★ ★ ★

Flora wasn't the kind of girl to make a fuss. Jack knew how upset she must be, and wished he could take back his thoughtless words. He made his way back to the party, noticing Gareth chatting to a blonde girl who he vaguely recognised from the department Dan worked in. Trudy approached as soon as she spotted him.

'Jack, are you two all right? Flora just flew past me, heading for the bathroom.'

'She's upset. I'm sure it's only a storm in a teacup.' He hated himself for making light of it.

Trudy frowned. 'Dare I ask if Gareth played any part in this? I saw him take her for a dance.'

Jack nodded. 'To be fair, I was nowhere near when that happened. I know he's a colleague of hers. He probably assumed she came on her own and, well, maybe he thought Flora was fair game.'

'Do you want me to have a word? Though he's attached himself to a colleague of my husband's now. I do hope he notices her wedding ring! She'll definitely put him in his place if he doesn't behave himself.'

'Thanks, Trudy, but I think it's best left now. It would be awful to cast a cloud over your party.' He looked around. 'Everyone's having a lovely time.'

'Except for you and Flora, that is. I'm so sorry, but thank you for taking the sensible approach. Everything I've heard from my husband tells me you're a lovely man. I was thrilled when Flora told me you two had got together.'

He nodded, fearful of confiding in someone he hardly knew, yet terrified of losing the girl who'd come to mean so much to him. Flora mixed with male colleagues and chatted to male passengers every time she arrived for work. Being a single dad, even with family backup, took a lot of effort, and he maybe hadn't paid as much attention to his lovely girlfriend as he might have.

'You look distraught,' said Trudy gently. 'Should I go after her? Lovers' tiffs are not unusual, you know. And she's a very attractive girl, Jack.'

'Tell me about it! Flora glows. I'm more of a slow burner,' he said, giving Trudy a wry grin.

She patted his arm. 'Don't put yourself down. Do you realise, Flora named you Mr Gorgeous when she first started looking out for you among her passengers?'

Jack felt a tiny ray of hope. Flora had never told him that. But the events of the evening had rocked his confidence.

'I was going to drive her home tonight, even though you'd kindly invited her to stay. The plan was for me to collect her tomorrow and drive her to my in-laws' place so she could meet my daughter again and get to know Ellie's grandparents.'

'And now you think this isn't going to happen? Who's the problem here, Jack? You or Flora?'

'I can't bear the thought of her no longer being in my life, but maybe she's not ready to . . . '

'*But* nothing!' Trudy snapped. 'Flora's no flirt, whereas Gareth is. Believe me, he's no threat to your happiness. She's fallen in love with you, Jack Slater and you'd better believe it. Now, will you wait here while I go and sort her out? Or will I be faced with her sobbing into her porridge tomorrow morning?'

20

Jack was driving Flora home through the twilight. Sitting quietly beside him, she decided the sky resembled an artist's palette. Pale blue, pastel pink, and rich plum shades dissolved into each other as the sun sank beyond the horizon.

'Thanks for saying you still wanted me to drive you home,' Jack said as he increased speed on the dual carriageway.

'Thank you for waiting while Trudy found me and talked sense into me. I didn't want you to leave the party with things the way they were.'

'I don't think either of us handled the situation very well. We're a sensitive pair, aren't we?' He reached for her hand and squeezed it.

Flora thought for a few moments. 'I've never been in love before, Jack.

I've heard people talk about being on a rollercoaster of emotions, and now I know exactly what they mean.'

'I acted very thoughtlessly this evening, and for that I apologise. To be honest, I couldn't quite believe how jealous I felt when I saw Gareth hustle you beneath that willow tree.'

She shuddered. 'Don't remind me. I don't think I was in any danger, but I was so relieved when you came to find me. He likes making conquests, and I don't play games like a lot of girls do.'

'There's no question about your loyalty, Flora. I still marvel at how you stayed with your farmer boyfriend for so long.'

'I shouldn't have done. But that's all in the past now. I just wonder if I'm too naïve for you.'

He laughed out loud. 'I'm sorry, my love. I think I'm the one feeling a tad inadequate here.'

'Well, you shouldn't. Some girls like those sweet-talking tall, dark and handsome types, but I'm not one of them.'

'In some ways, I've been taking you for granted, and that's not good. I'd like to make it up to you.'

'There's no need,' Flora said. 'We were getting on all right, weren't we? More than all right, I'd say!'

'I'm well aware I'm not your typical romantic hero. It took me a while to pluck up the courage to ask you out in the first place.'

Flora's heart melted. 'When you reach a convenient spot, could you please stop the car, so I can say something to you that I think needs saying?'

'Whatever you wish.'

Flora waited until they turned down the minor road leading to her home. Jack parked in the first layby they came to.

'You have my full attention,' he said, turning to look at her.

'Good,' Flora said. 'I understand what a tough time you've had over the last few years. In some ways I was coasting, sticking to the same job and marking time with a boyfriend who took me for granted while I let him do so.'

'I'm very glad he didn't ask you to marry him, Flora.'

'He did me a huge favour by not doing so. It would've been awful if I'd sleepwalked into marriage, Jack. Because if I had, I'd never have met you; never have known the joy of having your little girl put her hand in mine and start chatting away about her school and her toys and asking me if I had a princess dress and did I like baby ducklings.' She paused for breath. 'You and Ellie mean the world to me. I'll let you into a little secret now. When I first spotted you on the train, I gave you a special nickname. This is a bit embarrassing, but I called you Mr Gorgeous. I didn't realise how appropriate that name was.'

He chuckled. 'Now you're embarrassing me! Trudy let slip what you called me, but I'm afraid I didn't think up a name for you. I just kept on hoping I'd see you on the train, and if I didn't in the morning, I still hoped you'd be working on the evening one.'

'Thank goodness you decided to come and talk to me that morning when we were delayed. I want to say one important thing. If you still want me to meet Robbie and Megan tomorrow, I'm still happy to do so, even though I'll probably be shaking with nerves. I was devastated when you suggested you mightn't be exciting enough for me. That's simply not true. I'm not interested in the kind of excitement you might've been hinting at. I don't want a man like Gareth in my life — someone who I'll never know whether he'll be around next week or not. I want to feel loved and to love you back, and be free to give your little girl all the hugs and affection she deserves. I can't replace her mum, but I'll do my best to be as good a mum as I possibly can. That's about it, really.'

'Wow. That's amazing.' He shook his head slowly, a sweet smile transforming concern to tenderness. 'I don't know what on earth I've done to deserve you, but hearing you say all that makes me a very happy man.'

They hugged one another, each having a fit of the giggles when Jack accidentally beeped the horn with his elbow. They drove the rest of the way to Flora's home in contented silence.

★   ★   ★

Jack was back next afternoon minutes after Flora and her mother finished the washing up.

'I've brought Ellie with me,' he announced when Flora answered the doorbell. 'We can wait in the car till you're ready.' He leaned in for a kiss.

'Could you bring her inside? I'd love her to meet my parents.'

'Well, I'd very much like to meet your folks, so I'll ask her, shall I?'

'Let me!' Flora ran down the drive

and waved at the little girl before opening the car door. 'Darling, would you like to come in and meet my mum and dad? Your daddy's just saying hello to them.'

Ellie put her head to one side. 'Can I see your bedroom?'

'Of course! I still have my soft toys sitting on top of the wardrobe.' Flora unfastened the child's seatbelt so she could hop out of the car. The two walked hand in hand up to the house, Ellie chattering about what her grandma was planning to give them for tea, but suddenly clamming up when Flora's mother came forward.

'You must be Ellie,' Rose said, smiling at the little girl. 'Your daddy's talking to Flora's father. Let's all go inside, shall we?'

Flora heard the men chatting in the sitting room and held her hand out to Ellie again. 'We're going to visit my room so Ellie can see all my old soft toys.'

Rose Petersen laughed. 'Off you go,

then. I'll go and talk to Jack, shall I?'

'Yes, please do. We won't be long, Mum. I don't often get visitors wanting to see my old teddies, Ellie. They'll be delighted to meet you.' Flora led the way.

Ellie giggled. 'How many do you have?' She stomped up the stairs beside Flora.

'Five teddies and two fluffy rabbits.'

'Do they all have names?'

'Of course.' Flora opened her bedroom door. 'I'll lift them down for you.'

When the two arrived downstairs again, Ellie was cradling a beautiful Dutch doll in her arms. She ran towards her father, who turned round, a look of astonishment on his face.

'Daddy, look what Flora gave me! She's called Rosa.'

Jack looked warily at Flora. 'She must be one of your childhood treasures. Are you sure you want to give her away?'

'Positive. She was a gift from a great-aunt who hadn't seen me for ages and didn't realise I was already sixteen years of age.'

'Ah.' Jack's eyes twinkled. 'She must have got quite a surprise when she turned up and realised she'd brought the wrong kind of gift!'

'I pretended I collected dolls of different nationalities, so got round it that way.'

'Always a tactful girl, our Flora,' muttered her dad. 'Now, Jack, I gather you're a planning expert.'

'Dad . . . ' Flora warned, fearing Jack faced becoming lumbered with some problem she didn't know about.

'It's fine.' Jack winked at her. 'Is there something I can help with, sir?'

'Call me Colin, son. I'd appreciate your looking at the back room and seeing if you think a conservatory would be in order.' He whisked Jack away, leaving the women looking at each other in amazement.

'He must have taken to your boyfriend,' Rose whispered. 'Mind you, I'm not surprised.' She sat down beside

Ellie on the settee. 'Shall we talk about Rosa's dress? And do you know that Flora gave this pretty doll almost the same name as mine?'

* * *

'This has been a pretty full-on day,' Jack said as he drove Flora home, leaving Ellie with her grandma to have her bath and get into pyjamas ready for her bedtime story.

'The whole weekend's been quite, um, eventful!'

Flora shot him a mischievous glance. 'Though I've much preferred today's events to yesterday's.'

'I don't think we spoiled anyone's enjoyment of the party, except maybe Gareth's,' Jack said. 'Anyway, you certainly made a hit with Ellie's grandparents today, darling. I know it can't have been easy for you.'

Flora hesitated. 'I was a little anxious about meeting Megan and Robbie, of course I was. But once I got talking to them, they made me feel really at home.'

'They know how much you mean to me.'

'Thank you,' Flora said. 'I hope they understand how I feel about you and Ellie now.'

'Oh, I think they have a pretty good idea.' He reached for her hand and kissed her fingers before releasing them again. 'Quite honestly, I'd thought meeting your father might be more daunting than meeting your mum, but Colin couldn't wait to get me talking about man stuff!'

'He looked as if he'd won top prize on the Lottery! He really should have had a son to talk DIY with. Instead, he got me, the vintage clothes and doll lover.'

'Well, he must be thrilled that his little girl decided to become a train guard. Plus, you must be one of the most beautiful train guards in the country, if not the fairest one of all.'

'You flatterer! Seriously though, it's

been a lovely day, hasn't it?'

'It has. I forgot to say, my sister-in-law wants us to go to a barbeque at their place next Sunday afternoon. Do you think you'll be able to make it?'

'Hopefully. The person who asked me to swap schedules has promised to return the favour, so I'll contact her this evening and let you know. A barbeque sounds fun.'

'I'm waiting to hear from the vendors of the house we viewed. The agent tells me they had to make a sudden journey up north to visit an elderly relation who's gone into hospital.'

'That's sad for them. They've received your offer, I imagine?'

'It's been passed to them, but I expect I'll have to wait for them to return home. It's no big deal. I don't imagine Robbie and Megan will throw Ellie and me out while we wait to hear.'

Flora bit her lip. 'They're going to miss you terribly when the time comes. I picked that much up, and it's entirely understandable.'

Jack slowed down the car and pulled up in a layby. 'What'd we do without these places to stop in?' he joked as he cut the engine and turned to her.

'Is something wrong?'

'Nothing at all . . . but I think you should know I made the decision to buy a home of my own for Ellie and me, well before I met you. I don't want you to think that falling in love with you has influenced the way I feel about having my own place.' He put his arm around Flora's shoulders and she snuggled against him.

'One day,' he whispered against her ear, 'we'll have our romantic moments without a gearstick and steering wheel playing gooseberry. Now, young lady, I'd better get you home before your dad changes his mind about my suitability as a boyfriend for his only daughter.'

21

'I've given Gareth a piece of my mind,' Trudy said. She happened to be taking over from Flora on the early afternoon service the following Tuesday.

Flora pulled a face. 'I should've known better than to dance with him.'

'Nonsense! He was out of order, whether he knew Jack was around or not. I doubt he'll be on my guest list next time we have a party.'

'It was a lovely party. I'm so glad we've all met up. Jack and I were wondering if you and Dan would like to join us for a meal some time. Our treat.'

'Yes to meeting up, but you've no need to treat us.' Trudy glanced up at the big clock above the platform. 'I must get on board. But is everything all right between you two, now? No fallout after Saturday night, I hope.'

'Everything's great, except . . . '

'Except what? Oh my goodness, you can't leave me in suspense!'

'It's only a tiny concern, so why don't I email you? I'm probably worrying for nothing, but it'll do me good to get my thoughts down in writing.'

'If I can help, I will. Don't forget to get in touch. Take care!'

Trudy hoisted her wheelie case on board, already chatting to the attendant in charge of the refreshment trolley.

Flora walked slowly towards the mess room. Probably she shouldn't have said anything to her friend, but now she had, she would keep her word. Trudy was discreet, and it was good to have a confidant who'd known about Flora's feelings for Mr Gorgeous, long before she found out his real name and learnt he reciprocated.

Before she went any further, she checked her mobile phone and found she'd missed a message from Jack. He'd taken to texting her to say which train he planned to take that afternoon; and she, of course, always replied. This time, he was involved with a site visit and would be heading home on the later service. She swiftly sent a response. He'd become such an important part of her life, she couldn't imagine how she'd cope if he changed his mind about her. But, if she was entirely honest, the tiny worry she mentioned to Trudy had all the signs of building into a serious concern.

She felt relieved when she went to have a meal and met another female train guard in the cafeteria queue. They agreed to share a table, and Flora appreciated having someone to keep her mind off personal matters while on her break.

* * *

Flora's mum let her off helping wash up after the evening meal. 'Your dad's offered to do it,' Rose said. 'He knows my favourite cookery programme's on tonight. Do you fancy watching it with me?'

Flora shook her head. 'No, you're all right, Mum. You watch it in peace, and I'll go and deal with some emails I need to send.'

Her mother hesitated. 'You look a bit pale. I hope that job's not getting too much for you.'

'Some days are busier than others. You know that, Mum.'

'You haven't fallen out with Jack, have you? Your father and I quite took to him, but I suppose it's not quite the same if a man already has a child.'

Flora took a deep breath. She loved her mum to bits, but sometimes Rose could be a little too perceptive. Or did she mean intrusive? Flora hadn't fallen out with Jack, but was finding difficulty controlling the side of her that insisted on asking one very big question.

'I haven't seen him since the weekend, Mum. Don't worry, we haven't had a row.' She began climbing the stairs.

In her room, she switched on her laptop. Almost everyone she knew used a smartphone to do stuff Flora preferred to deal with on her laptop. Her friends were used to her by now, even if they couldn't understand her. This same tendency, which Jack shared, was one of the things that endeared him to her.

She began writing to Trudy.

Dear Trudy,

Here I am, as promised, to explain what's bothering me. You might think I'm trying to rush things but I'm not, truly I'm not. Jack has loads on his mind just now, trying to buy a house and having to wait while the vendors consider his offer, plus fitting in dates with me, helping his in-laws, and being around as much as possible for Ellie.

But here's the thing. We've taken a while to get to know each other and to own up about our feelings. You know how long I admired him until that amazing morning when he sat down with me to talk. I don't think I'll ever forget how happy it made me, hearing he felt about me as I felt about him.

We had a couple of dates but I knew he was delaying introducing me to his daughter and to Ellie's grandparents and I didn't blame him for that. Naturally, he'd be wary, even though it's a few years since he lost his wife. He's bound to have decided it might be asking too much to fall in love with someone who loved him back, and who was also prepared to share him with his little daughter.

I have no problem at all with Ellie. She's lovely, and I hope she feels the same way about me. Megan and Robbie, who are Jack's in-laws, seemed fine with me when Jack took me round to tea the day after your party.

Trudy, by now I bet you're thinking, what's Flora got to worry about? I'll try to explain. Jack seems to think that if he buys a house I'm happy with too, that means it'll be fine for me to go and live in it. As I said, he hasn't yet had his offer accepted, and maybe he'll need to forget that house and try to find another one that's suitable. What else can he do? But whichever house he ends up buying, I really feel I'd like to be part of the whole moving process. Does that seem unreasonable? I want to support him and Ellie, and the loveliest thing in the world would be for Jack and I to get married so we can all three move in together as a family. There, I've said it! I hope you'll understand and not think I'm asking too much.

Jack has hinted more than once that he has something important he'd like to ask me. I can only think he means a marriage proposal. We did have a falling-out last Saturday night, as you know, but that's the only time — and thanks to you, we each came down off our high horses and sorted things out. Sunday was a beautiful day. Everyone important to him and to me has been introduced now, except for his sister-in-law and her family. But we've been invited to a bar-becue at her place this coming weekend, so hopefully she won't take an instant dislike to me.

What worries me is that something's preventing Jack from proposing. He must surely know I love him and can't bear the thought of life without him! If there's a problem, why doesn't he come out with it so we can talk it through?

The other thing bothering me is how quickly he told me he worried he wasn't exciting enough for me. I found that very puzzling. I'm not the most exciting of people, as you well know. I feel as though I've known him forever, and I'm convinced we're soulmates, but maybe Jack doesn't feel the same and that's why he hasn't asked me to be his wife.

I'm sorry to pour all this out to you, but you did ask!

Love,

Flora xx

She pressed the Send key and sat staring at the screen, wishing life didn't have to be so complicated. If she closed her eyes and imagined she was in Jack's arms, maybe that would make her feel a little better. But maybe she'd be advised not to take a happy ending for granted. He'd learnt to cope without a wife. Was it asking too much to expect him to go through the whole engagement and marriage procedure again, with a different woman?

22

Today, Jack resolved, would be the day he plucked up courage and asked Flora to marry him. For that reason, he sent his usual weekday text message, but this time asking her which train journey westbound was scheduled to be her last of the day. When she sent him a message, saying she'd be working the service departing Wolf's Hill at five o'clock, he swiftly responded. *See you later*, he'd typed, not forgetting to add his love and a couple of kisses.

He worked through his lunch break so he could leave the office in time to catch Flora's train. Normally, he liked to have a plan in place. After all, town planning was his chosen career. But trying to map his life had seemed pointless between losing Charlotte and finding Flora, who'd come along just as he'd begun to feel that the best way forward would be for him to move into his own house. He knew it wouldn't be the easiest thing to do, but he was well aware he couldn't shelter behind Ellie's family for too much longer.

Now, months down the line, he knew he wanted Flora to be his wife. She'd talked very touchingly and honestly about how she'd deal with becoming Ellie's new mum, and he had no doubts about her sincerity. This hitch over his house purchase was a pain, but house buying was never a rose garden, and he was determined to find the right place before much longer. But it would be wonderful if only Flora could move in at the same time as he and Ellie.

So, if he proposed now, would Flora be pleased or not? Would she decide she needed more time in order to be totally sure of her feelings? She was younger than he was, although — he smiled at the thought — like him, she'd sooner stay home and talk to the potted plants than party all night. He loved the way she enjoyed the same simple treats to which he was accustomed.

But he was tired of trying to split himself in half in order to spend time with his daughter and his girlfriend. He was tired of sitting in his car, wishing they could all three be properly together. He was tired of snatched conversations and furtive kisses outside the guard's office while the train rattled along the track, and his heart beat faster and faster while he gazed at his lovely girlfriend, sometimes wishing they could stay on the train forever and forget everything else but themselves.

He felt a twinge of guilt for not including Ellie in this plan. Of course, she was important, and her welfare was his greatest consideration. But Ellie would grow into a teenager with a mind of her own. She'd train for a career, and her daddy would no longer have the same importance in her world. That was only right and proper.

But was it too much and too soon to

reach out for this chance of happiness with Flora? There was only one way to find out.

* * *

Flora read Trudy's response to her email before going to bed early. She thought about her friend's advice while snuggling down, her window wide open to the fields behind the house, as the evening had been warm. Trudy felt Flora was worrying too much. But she totally understood her friend's emotions, and felt she and Jack really needed a few days' break to get away from trains and family, no matter how dear their relations were to them. The more she thought about it, the more Flora liked the idea. But no way did she intend on suggesting Jack came away with her and left his daughter behind. That didn't sound right at all.

* * *

Jack's phone rang that afternoon while he stood on the platform, waiting for his train. At first he thought it might be Flora calling but he noticed the number belonged to his sister-in-law.

'Hi, Clare, what can I do for you?' He walked towards the quieter end of the platform, holding his phone close to his ear.

'Apologies if I'm interrupting you at work, Jack.'

'No, I'm waiting for my train home.'

'I wanted to ask you whether we could possibly borrow Ellie for a few days over half-term. That gorgeous holiday centre down the coast has had a cancellation, and we're on their waiting list. Two little girls will be easier to keep happy than one, believe me!'

'You want to take Ellie away with you? That's very kind.'

'As I said, I have an ulterior motive. You know we'll look after her and make sure she enjoys herself.'

'I'll ask her as soon as I get home, but I bet she says yes.'

'You won't delay? There's another little schoolfriend we could ask, but I'd prefer to take Ellie.'

'Well, let me answer for her and say yes please, make the booking. I'll ring you later — I don't want you to miss out on this.'

'Perfect! Speak soon.'

He closed the call just as the train's engine became visible in the distance. Jack always enjoyed this moment, knowing Flora was on board. And he'd just done something out of character! He'd made a snap decision on his daughter's behalf. Fine, people would doubtless laugh at him if they knew, but he'd thrown caution to the winds. And he was sure he'd done the right thing, and Ellie would be thrilled to bits.

He suddenly realised he'd moved to the wrong end of the platform, and began jogging back so he could board the last carriage. Flora needed to monitor the train from the rear so she could communicate with the train dispatcher, as this was a manned station.

He saw her opening the door and helping a passenger to disembark, and the feeling of joy was so great, he had to swallow hard and clear his throat.

Flora looked at him as he appeared beside her, her eyes solemn. 'You look different.'

'Do I? In what way?'

'I don't know. I'd have to think about it.' She stood aside to let him board. She was always so professional, and he wouldn't have it any other way.

'I'll come and find you later, after you've done your ticketing run.'

'I'll look forward to it.' She smiled at him.

Jack found a seat and sat staring through the window while doors banged and whistles sounded and the train set off again down the track towards its next destination. Flora smiled at him as she passed him on her way down the aisle. He looked at his watch and hoped she wouldn't take too long. Was he doing the right thing? Making an unexpected request while she was on duty? There was only one way to find out.

He made his way through the carriages until he reached the door marked Staff only and stood outside, one shoulder propped against the bulwark so he didn't lose his balance. Flora appeared a few moments later.

'Brilliant timing,' he said.

'I need to talk to you.' She gave him that solemn, green-eyed gaze again.

Jack longed to take her in his arms. Maybe this wasn't the most glamorous of places to choose for what he had in mind, but he couldn't wait.

'Flora, do you mind if I speak first? I don't think I can leave it any longer.'

'I feel the same.' She bit her lip. 'But you go on, then.'

He got down on one knee and reached for her hands. 'I love you very much, Flora. Will you do me the honour of becoming my wife?' He was trying hard not to sway too much.

Flora's mouth was a round O of surprise.

'Flora? I love you too much to lose you.'

She shook her head slowly. 'You won't lose me, Jack. Yes, of course I'll marry you! I'll marry you whenever you like.'

Jack lurched to his feet. 'Dare I kiss you?'

She looked around. 'One quick kiss!'

Their lips touched just as the door to the driver's cabin opened and one of the drivers appeared. He took one look at Flora and Jack and burst out laughing. 'Caught you,' he exclaimed.

'We've just got engaged,' Jack said, still holding on to Flora.

'Well, congratulations, sir,' said the driver. 'You've got yourself a lovely girl. I was about to tell you, Flora, we have to wait a few minutes at the next station. There'll be passengers joining us off a service that's delayed. If we don't pick 'em up, they'll have a long wait for the next train.' He disappeared back into the cabin.

'Extra time,' Jack whispered. 'Hey, darling, what's so funny?'

'You'll never guess,' she said. 'I'd made up my mind to ask you to marry me, but I wasn't sure I'd have the nerve to propose on the train.'

'I've been so worried you might feel I was rushing you,' Jack said.

'And I've been worried you might think I should take more time to decide. I don't need time, darling.'

'Could you get a few days' holiday at short notice?' Jack asked.

'Maybe. I'd have to ask. But, why?'

'It's half-term soon, and I have a few days' leave owing. But Ellie's been invited to join her auntie and family for a trip to that holiday place everyone's raving about. I thought it would be great if you and I could snatch a few days together before the house move.' He lowered his voice. 'And before the wedding.'

'Oh, Jack. I can't believe all this is happening!'

'Am I forgiven for proposing before you got the chance?'

'Definitely. You took me by surprise, Mr Gorgeous, and I couldn't be more delighted.' Flora put her arms around Jack and kissed him. 'I love you,' she said.

'And I love you.'